SWEE

Four years after they had separated,
Alix found herself forced to be once
again in the constant company of her
husband Kirby. But any idea of reconciliation soon vanished as Alix realised
that Kirby had chosen her successor . . .

SWEET HARVEST

BY
KERRY ALLYNE

MILLS & BOON LIMITED
17–19 FOLEY STREET
LONDON W1A 1DR

First published 1979
Australian copyright 1980
Philippine copyright 1980
This edition 1980

© Kerry Allyne 1979

ISBN 0 263 71372 3

Set in Linotype Times 11 on 13 pt.

Made and printed in Great Britain by
Richard Clay (The Chaucer Press), Ltd., Bungay, Suffolk

CHAPTER ONE

THE apathetic eyes of the girl lying so passively in the neatly made hospital bed suddenly came to bright, flaring blue-green life.

'What on earth made you contact him, of all people?' she demanded bitterly of the trim, greying-haired woman seated on the chair close beside her.

'You've been very ill, Alix, and—and I thought he had a right to know,' Mrs Ingram defended her actions to her daughter hastily. 'After all, he is your husband.'

'*Was!* Our marriage ended four years ago, remember?'

'Socially, perhaps, but not legally,' she was corrected firmly. 'Neither of you sought a divorce.'

'I couldn't afford to, and he probably couldn't be bothered,' Alix retorted with more feeling than she had shown for some months. 'Although why you should continue to think he has any rights at all where I'm concerned I don't know. Just because I've had pneumonia there was no need for you to panic into telling him. It's not as if I'm at death's door.'

'But Dr Burns hasn't been at all satisfied with your recovery, darling ... as you well know,' Mrs Ingram returned worriedly. 'When I spoke to him the day before yesterday he made the suggestion that, if it was at all possible, then an extended convalescence in a warmer climate could be just what you need.'

Alix's mouth turned down at the corners wryly. 'So you automatically thought of Kirby.'

'Well ...' Her mother spread her hands expressively wide. 'North Queensland does enjoy far more pleasant temperatures at this time of year. Canberra winters always seem never-ending.'

'They're still preferable to seeing him again,' came the flashing retaliation. 'I hope he turned the idea down flat!'

'Actually, he was very ...' a pause in order to select the right word, 'solicitous. We had quite a long talk on the phone the other night.'

'That must have cost you a fortune you couldn't afford!'

Mrs Ingram shook her head and smiled gently. 'No, after I'd explained why I was contacting him, he very thoughtfully suggested I hang up and then he rang me back so I wouldn't have to pay for the call.'

'Such generosity!' Alix quipped facetiously. 'His financial status must have improved considerably.'

'That's unkind, Alix! Kirby was more than willing to give you anything you set your heart on if it was within his power to do so.'

'Except his time!'

'The property was new and he was building it up ... for the two of you!' her mother reminded her with some asperity. 'You should have been grateful you had a man willing to work that hard for you, not everyone's so fortunate.'

Alix reached out a slender hand to clasp one of her mother's warmly. 'I know, Mum, I know,' she whispered contritely. When he was alive her father had been more than content to allow his wife to do the work of two while he spent his time devising impractical schemes which were supposedly guaranteed to make them rich overnight but only seemed to leave them poorer each time he tried putting them into practice.

'Maybe, at eighteen, I was just too young to know what marriage was all about,' she continued slowly. 'I just couldn't understand why he felt the need to work such long hours on his own place when his parents already had a property big enough to support both families and were quite willing to hand it over to him.'

'Perhaps pride of achievement had something to do with it,' Mrs Ingram suggested drily. 'Kirby Whitman certainly never struck me as a man who wanted anything handed to him on a plate.'

'And you think I did?' Alix questioned reproachfully.

'Well, I would hardly say six months was enough time to give your marriage a chance to work. When the first difficult situation arises, you don't run away, Alix, you try harder to overcome it.'

'I did try,' Alix contradicted indignantly, and moved restlessly beneath the covers. 'But—but it wasn't only that, there were other things that went wrong too. I wasn't the only one at fault. You always did think the sun shone out of Kirby and that he could do no wrong,' she complained.

'Not entirely, darling,' her mother sought to re-assure her earnestly. 'It's just that you've told me so little of what happened. Apart from a few references to "other things", you've hardly said a word about it since the day you arrived back at the apartment.'

Alix turned her head to stare across the other un-occupied bed in the room towards the open window. And nor would she be elaborating in the future either. It was too humiliating to even think about. The sus-taining light died out of her wide spaced eyes within their frame of dark lashes and she listlessly turned back again.

'You might at least have taken my word for it,' she sighed.

Mrs Ingram edged closer on her chair, asserting swiftly, 'But I did! Why else do you think I've ac-cepted your separation for all this time without say-ing anything?'

'Then phone him again when you get home and tell him I've made a rapid improvement and you're sorry for bothering him unnecessarily,' came the fretful plea.

'I can't do that, darling, I'm sorry. We need help to get you better.'

'But not *his*!' Tears glistened in Alix's eyes and her fingers clenched on the pristine white sheets. '*Please*, Mum,' she beseeched again, 'please ring him.'

'It—it's too late,' Mrs Ingram shook her head distractedly, somewhat nervous now of the events she had innocently set in motion. 'He'll be on his way, he said he would be leaving almost immediately.'

'No!' Alix gasped hoarsely, not wanting to believe what she had heard. 'Oh, God, how could you have done such a thing? You know how I feel about him!' Struggling into a sitting position she threw back the covers and swung her legs over the side of the bed. 'Well, I refuse to see him. I won't even be here, in fact, because I'll sign myself out right now.'

'Alix!' her mother shouted frantically, jumping to her feet and reaching for the pushbutton on the wall before hurrying around to the other side of the bed. 'You're not well enough to sign yourself out,' she advised anxiously, one hand closing around her daughter's arm. 'So do get back into bed, there's a good girl.'

Alix's mouth set in a stubborn line. 'No,' she refused with a sob, and slid her feet to the floor, only to find her legs so weak after such a long period of inactivity that they crumpled under her when she attempted to take her first steps. In despair she bowed her head and tears coursed down her cheeks. 'I won't see him, *I won't*!' she cried helplessly.

When the nurse arrived the situation was summed up at a glance and within a few minutes Alix had been helped back to bed, the doctor called, and a calming sedative given. Mrs Ingram stood by apprehensively and then spoke quietly to the doctor before he and the nurse left. By the time their conversation was finished Alix was gradually drifting into a

drowsy world of unconsciousness and it was an effort
for her to hold out a hand towards her parent. Mrs
Ingram clasped it between both of hers and sat on
the edge of the bed.

'I'm sorry, darling, I was only trying to do what I
thought best for you,' she explained sadly.

'I know, and I'm sorry too, for worrying you,' Alix
half smiled weakly, her eyelids beginning to droop.

'I'll ask Kirby not to—to come to the hospital,
then, shall I?'

Alix managed to summon a short mirthless laugh.
'After coming all this way, do you think a mere request is likely to stop him?'

'But if I ...'

'It ... doesn't ... matter,' Alix's head moved fractionally on the pillow, her words starting to slur. It
was becoming too much of an effort to even talk now.
'Maybe ... I ... I'll ...' With a sigh her eyes closed
completely and she gave up the fight against the inevitable, allowing waves of mind-cleansing sleep to
wash away her disquieting thoughts.

It was dark when Alix regained consciousness, her
wrist watch showing only ten minutes until the evening visiting hour, and she reached for her hair brush
with unsteady fingers to begin pulling it through her
tousled blonde hair. She had just finished applying a
light coating of pale pink lipstick when the night
nurse put her head around the door.

'We kept your dinner hot for you,' she smiled. 'I

think there's still time if you'd like it now.'

Eat? Alix had never felt less like it in her life!

'Not at the moment, thanks all the same,' she smiled back shakily. 'Although I wouldn't say no to a hot drink of some kind if you have it.'

'I'll see what I can do,' the other girl promised before she disappeared. It wasn't long before she was back again, a cup of tea in her hand. 'Sister had just made a pot in the common room, so it's freshly brewed,' she relayed triumphantly. 'Is there anything else I can get for you?'

'No, this is lovely, thank you,' Alix sipped at the hot liquid appreciatively. 'Shall I ring when I've finished it?'

'Please!' Twinkling brown eyes rolled meaningfully. 'Matron can't abide used china in the rooms when there's visitors around.'

Left on her own Alix drained the cup as quickly as she was able so the helpful nurse didn't get into trouble with her superior and then attempted to settle back on her pillows once it had been collected. As the hands on her watch crept inexorably towards the appointed hour, however, so her nerves tightened unbearably until they were like a quivering rope under tremendous strain. Her mouth was as dry as it had been before she'd had her drink and she was forced to grip her hands together fiercely in an endeavour to disguise her trepidation.

The forthcoming meeting with her husband—the first since she had so precipitately walked out on him four years ago—was assuming disastrous proportions within her mind and she could only hope that, when the time came, her mother would also accompany him into the room. She really didn't feel capable of facing him alone right at the moment.

The door swinging silently inwards had her catching her breath in her throat and clamping her teeth together firmly as a tall, commanding figure strode into the room bringing an impression of the wide open spaces with him. With a sinking heart Alix realised he was alone after all and licked at her dry lips nervously. His deeply tanned skin, cord pants, lemon roll-neck sweater, and brown check sports coat reminded her of an advertisement for the rugged outdoors and already she could feel her tiny store of defiance crumbling beneath the unspoken force of his personality as she stared at him without speaking.

He didn't appear to have altered much, she noted inconsequentially. The years from thirty to thirty-four seeming to have wrought far less change than hers from eighteen to twenty-two. He was still as lithe and attractive as he had been when they met. His dark brown hair as unruly, his firmly shaped mouth as lightly mocking, his vivid blue eyes as provoking.

'God, you look awful!'

The uncomplimentary exclamation cut into Alix's thoughts harshly and she closed her eyes to hide the anguish it created. When she opened them again it was to return his alert gaze with suspiciously bright eyes and trembling lips.

'How nice of you to say so, Kirby,' she laughed brokenly. 'But then you never did believe in mincing your words, did you? A spade was never anything else but a spade in your mind.'

'At least I always used to say exactly what I damned well meant,' he retorted savagely, his eyes assuming a frosty hue. 'I didn't lead *you* to believe everything was normal and then walk out on you the minute *your* back was turned!'

'Well, it certainly didn't appear to cause you too much concern at the time,' she remarked shakily. 'I noticed you never made any attempt to come after me.'

One well-shaped brow leapt upwards. 'Why the hell should I? If you'd wanted to come back you knew where to find me.'

'So I could compete for my own husband with— with *that* girl!' she choked. 'Oh, yes, you would have liked that, wouldn't you?'

'Her name's Melanie, not *that* girl, Alix, and your remark's still as bloody ridiculous as it was when you first made it four years ago!' he swore exasperatedly.

'Then why wouldn't you get rid of her when I asked you to?'

'Because she was a good secretary and I needed someone to handle that side of the business for me,' he returned coldly. 'It was obvious you had no intention of helping out.'

'I don't know anything about office work!' she cried.

'You could have learnt.'

'Who from ... you?' Alix queried acidly. 'You

were never there, so that just left dear little Melly and myself in the house .... oh, not forgetting her mother, of course! Between the two of them, one running the house and the other the office, there wasn't much *for* me to do. In fact, I used to feel like a guest in what was supposed to be my own home!'

Kirby thrust his hands deep into the pockets of his pants and expelled a long-drawn-out breath. 'If you did, you had nobody to blame but yourself. You could have taken over the running of the house from Clara ... if you'd wanted to.'

Alix very much doubted it. Clara Gordon had managed the two houses, Kirby's and her own, with such super-efficiency that Alix hadn't known quite how to suggest that she ought to take over. Consequently, she'd had more or less nothing to do all day except to wait for Kirby to come home, and after all those long hours spent on her own that had usually meant her reception was a dissatisfied and querulous one.

A couple of times she had accompanied him on those extended days spent clearing new paddocks, but as she neither had the knowledge nor the strength to help him in any way it had become a case of her having to sit and watch while he got on with the work. Eventually, she had come to resent the very land which gave him his living as it took so much of his attention and left so little time for her.

His suggestion that she might like to join some of the women's clubs in the nearest town and thereby get to know a few of their neighbours had been met with a resentful, 'I'm only eighteen, I don't want to spend all my days cooped up with a lot of stuffy old women discussing recipes and their children's latest illnesses!' He had tried explaining that wasn't the way it would be at all, but she hadn't been interested in listening and finally the matter had been dropped altogether.

Now she raised her eyes to Kirby's accusingly. 'The only thing I wanted was a little more of my husband's time.'

'So I remember you kept saying ... interminably!' His retaliation came callously, his expression bleak. 'But you were so damned selfish and possessive you weren't prepared to wait until I'd managed to get the place working. You wanted everything then and there, and if you couldn't have it, then to hell with me and our marriage!'

'That's not true!' Alix protested tearfully.

'Isn't it?'

'No!' Her fingers clenched together so sharply that her nails dug a series of half-moons into her palms. 'You seemed able to find the time to talk to Melanie easily enough!'

'Of course I did,' he rasped. 'It was important that I keep track of the paperwork involved too, you know.'

'Oh, naturally,' she attempted a despondent gibe. 'I was the only one unimportant enough to be ignored.'

A muscle jerked convulsively at the side of his taut jaw and he swung away to stand looking out of the window, broad shoulders flexing impassively. 'I suggest we agree to disagree on the past, Alix. There's not much point in raking up old grievances at this late date.'

Meaning he wasn't interested enough to care, Alix supposed miserably. But then why should he? No matter what he might have said to the contrary, she knew only too well how Melanie Gordon felt about him, and she couldn't envision that girl allowing the opportunity to usurp Alix's position to pass her by in her absence. It was probably a very satisfactory arrangement for Kirby. Conveniently married to one and having an affair with the other—no wonder he had never wanted a divorce!

As suddenly as he had turned away from her, Kirby now spun to face her appraisingly. 'How long have you had this pneumonia?' he finally asked.

Alix hunched one frail shoulder indifferently. 'A couple of months. It started out as one of those 'flu viruses that wouldn't respond to treatment.'

'And the doctor recommends you convalesce in a warmer climate?'

'So I believe,' she conceded reluctantly, and immediately shook her head as she continued, 'Although that needn't concern you. I'm sorry Mum bothered you with her call and you've wasted your time by coming down here, it really wasn't necessary. I—I might look terrible at the moment,' he had left her in no doubts in that regard, 'but I'm sure I can recuperate just as well in Canberra as I could anywhere else.'

'I doubt it.' He gave an involuntary shudder, making Alix realise that their low temperatures must have been doubly hard for him to take after north Queensland's winter warmth. 'I also doubt that you're more knowledgeable on the subject than your doctor is,' he went on bitingly. 'Besides which, if it means anything to you, your mother happens to be extremely worried about you.'

'Of course it means something to me,' she flashed resentfully. 'But that still didn't give her the right to contact you about it. What if we hadn't known anyone who lived somewhere warmer?'

'But as you do, the question is hardly relevant, is it?' He eyed her with insufferable irony. 'We may have separated, Alix, but in the eyes of the law you're still my wife and, therefore, my responsibility.'

'And as such I should be humbly grateful for your charity, I suppose?' she questioned tartly. 'Well, no thanks, I don't need your enforced benevolence. I'd much rather convalesce in my mother's apartment.'

'Unfortunately, however, in that regard you're forgetting one small, though very important, detail,' he taunted, and on seeing her looked of puzzled incomprehension, elucidated unsparingly, 'Your mother can't afford to keep both of you on her pension.'

Until now, it wasn't an aspect Alix had needed to consider and as a result her reply was flustered. 'I —I have some m-money of my own,' she stammered. 'I'm not exactly p-penniless, you know.'

'No?' He sounded extremely sceptical. 'So how much do you have? One hundred, two hundred, three hundred dollars?'

'It's none of your business,' she defied his right to ask. 'I have enough, that's all you need to know.'

'I'll be the judge of that!' he rapped, pacing towards the bed and towering over her threateningly. 'Exactly how much is *enough*, Alix?'

Weakened and exhausted by her illness, she had no resistance against such overwhelming forcefulness and unbidden tears began to seep past her eyelids, turning her eyes to the shimmering green of a tropical sea.

'S-stop b-bullying me, Kirby,' she quavered. 'You've got n-no right where I'm con-concerned any more.'

Undeterred by her plaintive evasion or her tears, he merely leant closer to reiterate his demand, 'How much, Alix?' with a firm hand capturing her chin so she couldn't avoid his brilliant blue probing gaze.

All too conscious of his touch on her flushed skin, Alix twisted out of his hold abruptly. 'Almost a hundred dollars,' she sighed, her brief surge of defiance evaporating.

Kirby stepped back from the bed, his hands coming to rest lightly on lean hips. 'And how long do you think you'll be able to manage on that?'

'Does it really matter?' she countered wearily. 'I'm sure you're not particularly interested in what happens to me. You're here because of a sense of duty.'

His lips thinned angrily. 'Blast you, Alix, don't make it any harder than it is already! I'm here because your mother said you needed help and, looking at you, I can see why she's been so worried. Good lord, girl, what have you been doing to yourself?'

'Well, what did you expect? I've been ill,' she cried defensively.

'For years by the look of it! My God, you're all hollows. Beneath your eyes, in your cheeks, round your collarbones . . . and you're as thin as a rake, to boot!'

'You're positive you haven't left anything out?' she questioned in a voice that shook from her efforts to keep her tone uncaring.

'Only that I feel like slapping some of that pigheadedness out of you,' he returned roughly. 'But you look so damned fragile I'm frightened you'd break in half if I did.'

'Well, perhaps you can take a raincheck on it,' she proposed huskily.

'I'd like to, believe me, but . . .' He broke off as Mrs Ingram hesitantly entered the room.

'Is it all settled, Kirby?' she asked.

'Just about, Grace,' he replied easily, standing back and motioning for her to take the chair he hadn't bothered to use. 'I'll be seeing the doctor before I leave this evening, of course, but I think you can take it as final that we'll be departing first thing in the morning.'

She sank down on to the chair with evident relief. 'Oh, I'm so pleased,' she smiled. 'I thought . . .'

'And just who is supposed to be leaving for where?' interrupted Alix stonily.

'Why, you and Kirby, of course, darling,' her mother explained in some surprise. 'He's taking you back to Maiyatta with him.'

'Not to my knowledge, he isn't,' Alix retorted.

'But—but ...' A calming hand was laid on Mrs Ingram's shoulder and she subsided thankfully.

'Oh, yes, I am!' Kirby's eyes bored into Alix relentlessly. 'I think you've caused your mother quite enough concern without expecting her to nurse you back to health as well.'

Which wasn't a sentiment Alix could dispute. Instead, she suggested, 'In that case, I'll go back to work on a casual basis until I'm well enough to be employed full-time.'

'Hah!' he snorted contemptuously. 'I doubt you could even manage that in your present state.'

'Kirby's quite right, darling,' Mrs Ingram added her own warning to that of her son-in-law. 'If you remember, you couldn't even walk when you got out of bed this afternoon.'

How could she forget? thought Alix dismally. It had been a last desperate attempt to escape this meeting with her husband. Now it seemed as though even her own body was conspiring against her.

'My summer clothes are all packed away,' she said at last. If she wasn't to be given any choice in the matter then she would put as many difficulties in his path as she possibly could.

'I got them all out and pressed them for you this afternoon,' her mother informed her in such a bright tone that Alix closed her eyes in despair.

'But I've lost so much weight they won't fit me now.'

'All the more incentive for you to make a rapid recovery,' inserted Kirby coolly.

'And what do you suggest I do in the meantime?' Her brows rose goadingly. 'Go around looking like a walking scarecrow?'

By way of an answer Kirby withdrew a cheque book from his coat pocket, wrote in it swiftly, and tearing out one leaf tossed it on to the bed.

'Buy some new ones,' he ordered through clenched teeth.

Not that she had any intention of using his money, Alix still raised innocent eyes to query, 'Where? They don't have a dress shop in the hospital.'

Kirby uttered a smothered exclamation and ran an exasperated hand through his hair, leaving it to Mrs Ingram to propose hastily, 'Perhaps I could buy a couple for you in the morning before you leave?'

'I don't know what size I am any more,' Alix murmured unhelpfully.

'We'll stop somewhere en route,' Kirby re-entered the conversation with a scarcely concealed sigh. 'You probably aren't strong enough to make the journey in one go anyway.'

Alix bit at her lip sorrowfully. 'I don't want to be any trouble.'

'No, I'm sure you don't,' he replied in the same pseudo-grieving tone. 'But a few hours in Brisbane and an overnight stop in Bundaberg or Rockhampton should make the trip more comfortable.'

'Maybe it would be easier if I just followed you in

a few days' time,' she now put forward hopefully, but the foreboding look he slanted at her from beneath lowering brows told her extremely clearly what he thought of that suggestion and she shrugged disappointedly, 'Oh, well, it was only a thought.'

What was left of the visiting hour was spent in Kirby and Mrs Ingram making their arrangements for the morrow. Alix's contribution was very small. All she had to do was to make sure she was ready when Kirby called to collect her and take her out to the airport. Apparently he flew his own plane these days instead of his father's, causing Alix to ponder deeply over the other changes that must have taken place at Maiyatta since she left.

Thoughts which had her tossing and turning restlessly long into the night after Kirby and her mother had departed, and railing futilely against the fates which had prompted her doctor to remark that he thought a warmer climate would be beneficial to her.

CHAPTER TWO

GRACE INGRAM arrived at the hospital early the following morning in order to help Alix dress and pack her few belongings in the small case she had brought with her.

'I thought a pair of slacks and a light cotton shirt, together with a thick jumper and your winter coat, would be best for you to travel in, then you can strip off layer by layer as you move northwards,' she explained brightly.

Sitting on the edge of the bed Alix surveyed her clothes uninterestedly. She didn't particularly care what she wore. 'I hope you brought some safety pins with you, otherwise I'll never keep my jeans on,' was her only comment.

Her mother held the pale blue denims up against her consideringly. 'Mmm, you are terribly thin, aren't you? Never mind, though, I expect they'll fit you again perfectly within a few weeks.'

Alix paused to wonder why her mother should choose to believe such a time spent in her husband's company would make so much difference to her well-being, especially since it should have been perfectly clear they weren't even on amicable terms, let alone loving ones, but she forbore to say anything lest she

23

spoil her parent's obvious pleasure and relief at seeing her daughter supposedly following doctor's orders. Alix was, in actual fact, pleased to know the load had been lifted from her mother's shoulders. Her only objection was to the person who had assumed the burden in her mother's place!

'Here, let me do that for you,' Mrs Ingram hurried to take the hairbrush from her daughter's hand once she was dressed and began brushing out the shoulder-length blonde hair with long soothing strokes in an attempt to put some life back into the now lustreless curls.

Alix pulled a wry face. 'I'm not that weak that I can't even brush my own hair, Mum,' she half smiled.

'I know, darling.' A stray curl was tucked tidily behind one ear. 'But it will probably be a while before I see you again and I'm just prolonging our parting.'

'Not as long as you think, if I have anything to do with it,' muttered Alix direfully.

'Now, Alix,' her mother remonstrated anxiously. 'Don't do anything silly, like coming back before you're fully recovered, will you?'

'Oh, I don't think you need have any worries on that score,' came the rueful reply. 'I'm sure my dear husband won't allow me to leave until I'm a hundred per cent fit. Someone might choose to think it was a reflection of his treatment of me otherwise.'

Mrs Ingram sighed and sat on the bed beside her, holding a slim-fingered hand. 'Oh, Alix, I do wish you didn't feel quite so bitter towards Kirby. You know, he didn't hesitate when I told him you needed help, and feeling like you do won't make recuperation any easier.'

Alix felt like saying she ought to have thought of that before contacting him, but she didn't, she held her peace and merely hunched her shoulders indifferently. It wasn't really her mother's fault. She had only turned to the person she considered most likely to aid them in a time of stress.

A peremptory knock on the door heralded Kirby's arrival as he walked into the room without waiting for an answer and stood, wind-tousled and flagrantly male, appraising their state of preparedness with alert eyes.

'Good, you're ready,' he remarked briskly, and strode towards the bed. 'Can you walk, or would you prefer a wheelchair?'

Alix drew in a deep breath and glared at him resentfully. 'I am *not* an invalid,' she snapped. 'With the support of my mother's arm, I shall *walk*, if you don't mind!'

In one swift movement he had scooped her off the bed and high into his arms, bearing her weight effortlessly. 'Sorry, my love—hell, holding you is like carrying a load of fairy floss—but there's no time for doing things slowly. I want to be away as soon as possible,' he advised authoritatively, then turned to Mrs Ingram to reveal, 'I settled Alix's accounts with the doctor and the hospital on my way in, so there's no call for any worries in that direction, Grace.'

'You had no right . . .!' Alix started to cut across her mother's grateful appreciation, only to be interrupted herself by a withering, 'Shut up! I did it for your mother's peace of mind, not for you!' which had her holding herself stiffly away from him and two bright flashes of colour marking her pale cheeks.

She didn't speak again until they had left the hospital and driven her mother home to her apartment, and then only in slightly tearful and disjointed sentences as she bade her goodbye and it really came home to her that she would be spending the remainder of the winter surrounded by people who wouldn't have been worried if they had never seen her again or not. It was a discomfiting thought and on the way to the airport she tried to dislodge it from her mind by staring out of the window and mentally ticking off the various landmarks and suburbs they passed.

The overnight frost still lay heavily on the ground and the deciduous trees looked stark and bare as their tangled branches stretched upwards into the pale blue sky. Unconsciously the scenes provoked memories Alix would rather have forgotten, but when it proved impossible to ignore them any longer she sighed and allowed them to flood back into her mind with an almost masochistic pleasure.

It had been winter too when she first met Kirby. On a day very much like this one, she recalled wistfully. He had been in Canberra to attend an old friend's wedding and she had been filling in the last week of her holidays after a skiing trip to Perisher Valley.

They had shared the same table for lunch in a small cafeteria one day when Kirby had decided to do some sightseeing, and Alix hadn't been able to keep her eyes away from him. Of course he had been older than any of the men she had been out with up to that time, but that had only seemed to add to his attraction. He was assured, commanding, rugged ... and he exuded a male magnetism she found captivatingly difficult to resist. When he spoke to her and it appeared he wasn't exactly impervious to her either, she had thought the bubble of excitement inside her would suffocate her with its magnitude.

That afternoon had been the most delightful in her young life, and she had willingly acted as Kirby's guide in showing him the sights. They had visited Black Mountain Lookout with its sweeping views over the Botanic Gardens, Lake Burley Griffin, and the city itself; the imposing War Memorial and the National Library; Blundell's Farmhouse, still furnished as it had been during the last century; Parliament House and the Prime Minister's Lodge; and the Royal Australian Mint where they had watched some of the nation's coins being manufactured. Though, in truth, neither of them had been more than mildly interested in what they saw, their greatest enjoyment had come from just being together.

Alix knew she had fallen head over heels in love before the week was out. She was on top of the world when they were together and restless and moody when they were apart. The only dark spot on her horizon was Kirby's impending departure, but when he told her he had delayed it for another fortnight she had been ecstatic at the news, for although she had grudgingly been forced to return to work she still saw him every lunchtime and they spent all their evenings in each other's company.

Two days before Kirby was due to leave he asked her to marry him, and Alix had agreed joyfully. It seemed all her dreams had come true at the one time and that nothing could possibly mar her happiness again. They were married the following day with only her mother and a few very close friends as witnesses and then they headed north to Townsville to break the news to Kirby's parents, who had been openly delighted with their new daughter-in-law, before continuing on to Maiyatta.

Maiyatta, Alix repeated with a sigh, and moved in her seat. That was where all her troubles had started. What with Melanie Gordon openly hostile at her presence—at least when Kirby wasn't around—and telling her that even though he had been momentarily persuaded into marrying Alix they were still more than friends, her dream world had suddenly but inexorably begun to shatter. Towards the end she had accused Kirby of marrying her only because he couldn't get her into bed any other way, but to her despair and utter humiliation, he hadn't bothered to deny it. He had merely given her a look of frozen disdain and grated, 'Then I got a damned poor bargain, didn't I?' as he stalked out of their bedroom. Three days later, after having tried to bring up the subject again and been summarily snubbed, she had angrily packed her bags and walked out.

And now, not of her own volition, she was returning. But to what? An alienated husband? This time there wasn't even any joy at the start!

Alix shook her head to clear her thoughts and frowned as she detected something familiar about the park they were passing. Abruptly, the recollection returned. They had fed the ducks there one afternoon during those first exciting weeks, laughing and pretending to argue as to who should be the one to throw out the last piece of bread. Without stopping to think she turned to Kirby with the words, 'Do you remember when...' forming on her lips, but as his eyes never wavered from the road and he displayed no recognition of their whereabouts, she slumped back again dejectedly. Even if he had remembered she doubted he would want to be reminded of it now!

At the airport she waited beside the car while Kirby carried their cases out to his sleek little Piper and then checked with the office that they were all set to leave. When he returned she was already making her way out on to the tarmac with slow faltering steps.

'No, please!' she entreated swiftly, her fingers clutching at his coat sleeve when he made as if to pick her up again. 'Please let me walk. I feel such a fool having to be carried.'

For an instant as he stood there looking down into her aquamarine eyes, large with pleading, and the wind viciously undid Mrs Ingram's handiwork as it whipped long strands of her hair across her face, Alix thought he meant to ignore her plea in the interests of haste. Then he shrugged, as if losing interest in the matter, and offered her his arm instead, which she held on to gratefully.

Even so, by the time they made it to the plane Alix was unbelievably tired but desperately trying not to show it. After eight weeks in bed and an enormous loss of weight she had no energy at all and when Kirby settled her in her seat she sank back against it weakly, too exhausted to even loosen her coat.

'I knew I should have carried you!' Kirby's voice lashed at her angrily as he leant across to buckle her seatbelt himself before attending to his own. 'Well, you can say goodbye to your shopping spree in Brisbane for that prideful effort, you little idiot! You wouldn't have the strength to walk into a shop now, let alone stand there trying dresses on.'

As she hadn't meant to spend his money anyway, it was no loss to Alix, but she hated to be so helpless and struggled a little further upright in an attempt to appear more her normal self.

'It—it's only temporary ... until I get my breath back,' she protested unsteadily. 'I'm over it now ... see?'

'What I *see* I don't think you would care to hear,' he retorted savagely, picking up the handpiece of his radio. 'So why don't you just collapse back in your seat like you were before and cut the acting, hmm?'

'Oh, God, I hate you!' she breathed scathingly. 'You really are a merciless bastard, aren't you?'

His eyes were as cold as the wind buffeting the plane. 'If I am, then perhaps you should be prepared to take some of the credit, Alix, because you sure as hell didn't leave me with very tender memories of you!'

'So why the feigned interest in my welfare now?' she demanded anguishedly. 'To give you an opportunity to pay off old scores?'

'No, as a favour to your mother, because I happen to think she deserves better than to spend her time fretting over her selfish and uncaring daughter!'

'I am not selfish and uncaring!'

'That's a matter of opinion!' His brows peaked with the taunt. 'But what would you call it when, rather than accept help from your husband, you would prefer to place an unbearable strain on both your mother's resources and health?'

'I'd call it preferring the frying pan to the fire,' she retaliated fiercely. 'But that's something you don't have to worry about, isn't it, Kirby? As long as you can dictate the terms you're happy, and be damned if they don't suit anyone else! You're the worst type of male chauvinist there is!'

'And you, my love, are the most petulant and self-absorbed virago I've ever come across!' he denounced with such sarcastic derision that Alix could only stare at him desolately, her throat working convulsively.

While he spoke to the control tower her thoughts

turned inwards. Was that really the impression he had of her? It was a perturbing revelation, although, she supposed sadly, considering the bitterness which had preceded their separation, it was one she should have been prepared for. What she couldn't understand, however, was the reason his condemnation should have hurt quite so much. After all, it wasn't as if she was still in love with him. She had managed to recover from the torment of that emotion long ago. The proof of her immunity being the fact that she had occasionally dated other men—attractive and desirable men—since the breakdown of her disastrous marriage, but not once had they come close to igniting even the smallest spark of desire on her part. She made sure her heart was securely encased within an impenetrable wall of indifference these days. No more the rapture and the wretchedness of love for her!

Immediately they were airborne Alix unbuckled her seatbelt, undid the buttons on her coat, and began searching through her bag for a cigarette. Normally she smoked very rarely, but right at the moment she desperately felt the need for something to pacify her jangled nerves. On discovering a somewhat crumpled packet lodged in one corner she extracted it thankfully, but on looking up, found Kirby's narrowed gaze watching her every move.

'When did you stop wearing your rings, Alix?' he questioned curtly.

Determined not to allow him to disturb her so easily again, she lifted one shoulder unconcernedly.

'When I reverted to using my maiden name.'

'Which was the day you left Maiyatta, I suppose?'

Alix cupped her hand around a match flame and applied it to the tip of her cigarette, drawing on it gently but pleasurably. 'No, it was about two days after that.' Actually, it had been a lot longer—more like two years than two days—but she didn't intend to tell him that.

With a muffled expletive Kirby's eyes came to rest on her cigarette. 'Don't you think your lungs have suffered enough punishment for a while without that?' he rasped contemptuously.

'You smoke—or at least, you did—and what I do with my lungs is nobody's business but my own,' she rounded on him, irritated because she knew his remark to have made sense. 'If I want to smoke, I will, and there's not much you can do about it.'

'I wouldn't be too confident of that,' he retorted mockingly. 'You seem to forget you were released into my care.'

'And, as usual, you seem to be confusing care with control,' she gibed back, her lips curving provokingly as she went on to taunt, 'But do tell me how you mean to enforce all the petty little regulations I'm sure you plan to devise? Am I to be handcuffed to you day and night?'

'Not at all.' His eyes slid over her consideringly from head to toe and his ensuing expression told her, more crushingly than words could ever have done, that she had been found wanting. 'I prefer to reserve my nights for pleasure and relaxation and you, my love, just wouldn't fit into that category at all,' he drawled.

'No?' she managed finally, with a pout of pretended disappointment. 'Oh, well, I wouldn't have wanted to intrude on Melanie's preserves anyway,' she sighed. 'I suppose she's still with you and that she was terribly disappointed,' malevolent, most probably, 'to hear that you considered it your christian duty to offer succour to your poor ailing wife in her hour of need.'

'As a matter of fact, I didn't have an opportunity to tell her.'

'Oh, dear, then you are in trouble, aren't you?' she laughed for the first time since she couldn't remember when, her blue-green eyes glistening with a mocking sparkle. 'Just think—on a sudden impulse—to show how strongly she disagrees with your decision, she might even be tempted to hand in her resignation.' And what a wholly satisfying thought that was!

'Okay, Alix, you've had your fun, now how about leaving Melanie out of this?' he recommended in an ominously low tone which she chose to ignore.

'But I couldn't possibly think of your home without including sweet capable Melly too,' Alix smiled with honeyed artlessness. 'I mean to say, it would be out of the question for you to keep the property going without her, wouldn't it?'

'That's the truth!'

'Well, there you are, then,' she continued recklessly. 'How could you expect me to ... Oh, you savage!

You're breaking my arm!' she broke off to protest loudly as her wrist was seized in a bone-shattering grip and she was hauled halfway out of her seat towards him.

'I said, *cut it out*, Alix!' he ordered irately, electric blue eyes blazing into hers fiercely, his voice as sharp as a razor's edge. 'Just count yourself lucky I'm flying this thing, otherwise you could have received worse!' disdainfully flinging her back into her seat.

Alix rubbed at the livid red marks Kirby's fingers had made on her skin, her eyes flickering doubtfully over his grimly set profile, her soft bottom lip held between small white teeth. Apparently any criticism of Melanie was strictly off limits, she reflected forlornly. If she had needed any evidence to prove in which direction his loyalties lay he had certainly given it to her in abundance today.

Covertly, she continued her searching scrutiny, noting the smooth bronze texture of his skin, the inflexible angle of his chin, the length of his luxuriant black eyelashes. In the pit of her stomach there was the first faint stirring of instinctive attraction and she suppressed it immediately in panic. She had enough problems without imprudently adding physical appeal to their number!

They refuelled at Coffs Harbour on the coast and took a taxi the short distance in to town for something to eat and drink. Their conversation had been practically non-existent since their dispute over Melanie, except for a few absolute necessities, and it continued that way until they were well over the border and into the Sunshine State.

The sun was still reasonably high when they began to circle Bundaberg preparatory to making their overnight stop and Alix was glad they had discarded their coats and jumpers some time back as the temperature was noticeably warmer. Kirby booked them in at one of the hotels in town and after seeing her to her room on the first floor turned to leave.

'It will probably be easier for you to have room service send up something for dinner instead of making the trip downstairs again,' he suggested at the door.

Blue-green eyes turned wistfully to the view of the city from the balcony doors—after having been cooped up in hospital for so long Alix had been looking forward to becoming a part of the great wide world again—and then she lowered them to the mottled green carpet.

'All right,' she agreed in a small voice. Looking the way she did, he no doubt wasn't overly anxious to be seen with her anyway.

Kirby ran a hand irritatedly around the back of his neck. 'Oh, hell, I don't know why I let you do these things to me. You get me stirred up quicker than a hornet does a beehive!' he sighed defeatedly. 'Okay, I'll collect you in about an hour for dinner. Can you manage on your own?'

'Yes, I think so, thank you,' she answered politely, and was surprised to see his well-cut mouth curve into the lazily attractive smile she had once known so well.

'Don't be too courteous, my love,' he counselled drily, 'or I might mistakenly believe it's the right girl I've got with me.'

Alix experienced a moment of shocking desolation and it was inconceivable for her to answer brightly. 'I'm sorry, I haven't been very grateful, have I?' she murmured .

'I'm not doing it for your gratitude!' Kirby's reply was short and to the point.

'No, that's right, I was forgetting, it was as a favour to my mother.'

For a time she thought he meant to add something further, but then he suddenly shrugged and opened the door leading into the hallway. 'I'll see you about seven,' he advised flatly before leaving.

It took Alix far longer than she had anticipated to have a shower and don a deep rose dress of corded silk. She felt stronger than she had that morning when walking out to the plane, but her legs were still very shaky and, annoyingly, she found it necessary to stop and rest every so often. A touch of tinted foundation did wonders to disguise the mauve smudges beneath her eyes and the hollows below her cheekbones, while a bright lipstick relieved the paleness of her complexion. A dab of faint perfume behind her ears and on each wrist completed her toilette, except that she hadn't yet been able to reach around to close the zip at the back of her dress, and she was still struggling to rectify the matter when Kirby returned.

'Mmm, you're getting some colour back into your

face,' he approved when she opened the door to him, and Alix didn't know whether that was a compliment to her handiwork or if it was a premature blush tinting her skin at the thought of having to ask him to help with her zipper.

Still standing close to the door, Kirby held one arm invitingly wide. 'If you're ready . . .?'

'In a minute,' Alix flushed fierily now, pointing over her shoulder. 'Would—would you mind?' she stammered embarrassedly, and turned her back to him. 'I couldn't reach it.'

'Quite like old times,' he remarked conversationally, stepping forward, but on coming closer a double crease appeared between his brows and he ran his fingers clinically over her prominently exposed backbone. 'Good grief, you're nothing but skin and bones! No wonder you find it exhausting just to walk. A strong wind would have no trouble in blowing you away right at the moment.' He ran the revealing zip swiftly up into place.

Alix spun to face him quickly. 'I—I never was heavily built,' she objected unsteadily, still remembering the feel of his hand on her skin.

'You don't have to tell *me* how you were built,' he reminded her wryly. 'My memory's not so bad that I've forgotten. You used to curve very nicely in all the right places—you definitely were not as shapeless as a piece of cardboard.'

'Like I am now, you mean?' she tried to shrug off the unattractive description casually. 'If you're not careful you'll turn my head with all your flattery.'

Unexpectedly, Kirby smoothed a hand gently over her soft cheek. 'I'm sorry, I guess I have been pretty thoughtless.'

The sudden change to consideration for her feelings caught Alix totally unprepared and, to her dismay, tears started to gather at the corners of her eyes. 'It doesn't matter,' she whispered throatily, shaking her head. 'All your comments have been perfectly true. I am shapeless and . . .'

'Feeling extremely sorry for yourself,' his voice hardened ruthlessly.

'I am not!' she flared, her tears drying immediately.

'It certainly sounded like it to me.'

'Only because you're all too ready and willing to find fault in whatever I say or do!'

'Is that so?' he gibed sardonically. 'Maybe I consider I have good reason.'

'Because I wasn't afraid to tell you a few home truths four years ago?' she scoffed.

'So that's what they were!' His voice dripped with sarcasm. 'I thought they were the peevish bitchings of a spoiled child.'

'Thereby giving you the chance to dismiss them as trivial! Well, I may have been young, Kirby, but I wasn't *that* young I didn't know what was going on behind my back!' she retorted.

'Meaning?' he growled.

'You know damned well what I mean!' Alix fired resentfully, her gaze locked stormily with his. 'You and Melanie, that's what! I knew what was going on with you two.'

'Then there was no point in your continually questioning me about it, was there?' he returned arrogantly.

'No point . . . !' she gasped, outraged. She knew men liked to consider they weren't naturally monogamous, but that he should have automatically assumed she would be willing to share him with another woman was unbelievable! Preparing to tell him exactly what she thought of such amoral principles Alix abruptly exhaled a deep breath, her simmering indignation going off the boil. Was there really anything to be gained by raking up painful reminders of the past? They were separated now and both obviously happy to be that way. Wasn't it better just to charge the whole distasteful episode to experience and then try to forget it? 'You're probably right,' she sighed an answer to his question at last. 'Certainly nothing is likely to be achieved by our fighting over it at this late date.'

Kirby's head dipped in satisfied acknowledgment. 'Now may we go to dinner?' he queried ironically.

'If you like.' Alix's agreement was given indifferently. For some inexplicable reason her previous anticipation had faded to such an extent she couldn't have cared less now whether she ate in her room or not. 'Are we going to the hotel dining room?' she asked for want of something better to say as she preceded him into the hallway.

'I thought it best.' The door was closed decisively behind them. 'You need an early night, so there didn't seem much reason to look further afield.'

'No, of course not.' And especially when his first choice had been to dine alone!

CHAPTER THREE

ALIX was awake early in the morning, having been conditioned to the habit by her weeks in the hospital, and her contented stretching was brought about more from being away from that sterile, regulated atmosphere than with enjoyment for her present whereabouts. Lazily, she listened to the first rumblings of traffic in the street below, her thoughts returning involuntarily to the night before.

She'd had no complaints about the food or Kirby's company—both had been adequate without being overdone—but something had been lacking all the same. Maybe it was their verbal sparring she missed, Alix grinned ruefully to herself, because that had definitely been kept to a minimum, by both of them. It had been a somewhat strained truce, though, she recalled, with each coming close to breaking it on a number of occasions when tempers had flared and then been controlled with difficulty. They were like a pair of duellists, testing out each other's defences before striking hard and then retreating to seek out another area of vulnerability.

With a sigh she tossed back the bedclothes and slid her long slender legs to the floor. Today would mark her return to Maiyatta and a reunion with Melanie

Gordon, and she wanted to be fully prepared for both.

When Kirby arrived after breakfast, in order to conserve her strength she had been quite willing to go along with his suggestion that it would save time if they had that meal in their rooms, Alix was already waiting for him. In pale lilac slacks with a matching check blouse, her make-up artfully applied, she knew she looked a far different picture from the girl he had collected from the hospital yesterday and her eyes sparkled with a little more confidence when she noticed his gaze turn appreciative, but only momentarily, at his first sight of her.

Striding purposefully into the room, he swung to fix her with a penetrating look from watchful blue eyes. 'Do you have your rings with you?'

'I'm sorry?' Alix frowned her bafflement and then, as realisation came to her, 'Oh, those rings!' Her eyes strayed to her bag resting on the bed. Although she never wore them, she did always carry them with her, but he wasn't to know that and she prevaricated nervously, 'N-no, they're at home.'

The look he gave her before snatching up her bag and emptying the contents violently over the bedspread was filled with animosity and she guessed he must have correctly interpreted her hasty glance. Swiftly he sorted through her belongings and, on finding nothing, gave his attention to the bag once again. Seconds later, from one of the inside pockets, he produced a small tissue-wrapped bundle which he threw on to the bed.

'While you're at Maiyatta you'll wear them, do you hear?' he rapped at her autocratically.

'I—I . . . what's the point?' she questioned through taut lips. 'We're not married any more.'

'We are in name, if not in fact, and while you're living in my house you'll wear the rings I gave you!'

Alix hunched one shoulder imperceptibly. 'My fingers are so much thinner now they're likely to fall off.'

Catching hold of her left hand, Kirby unwrapped the tissue paper himself and roughly thrust the two golden bands on to her third finger. 'I don't particularly care if you have to tie the damned things on, but you'll wear them just the same,' he grated.

'Anyone w-would think you were anxious to proclaim me as your w-wife,' she half laughed, half cried, dropping her gaze to the brilliant twinkle of her engagement ring—only one day older than her wedding ring. Their presence felt strange after so long without them.

'Then they would be wrong, wouldn't they?' he jeered callously. 'I happen to care for appearances, that's all. Make no mistake, Alix, my desire to have you back in my life is as non-existent as your desire to be here.'

The sting in his tone left Alix in no doubt that he mean every word and she wheeled away quickly to begin pushing her bits and pieces back into her bag. When she had finished she came upright with her head held high.

'Shall we go?' She tried to sound as if his total and utter rejection had made no impression on her at all.

Kirby bent to pick up the one small case she had brought into the hotel with her and motioned towards the door. 'After you, my love,' he taunted, and Alix stormed out of the room ahead of him, determined to make it downstairs on her own.

Today they landed at Mackay to refuel. Known as the "Sugar Capital of Australia" with its eight surrounding mills and the world's largest bulk sugar terminal—even without its half-completed extensions —it was an attractive town sited near the mouth of the Pioneer River with wide streets divided by picturesque garden beds and avenues of Royal Palms.

When they left the city behind and followed the coastline north, Alix had no eyes for the glorious scenery below them—long white breakers rolling on to sandy coastal beaches and, away towards the horizon, tiny green islands surrounded by clear coral lagoons—but sat twisting her rings agitatedly around her finger.

'Will you be landing at Townsville?' she asked eventually.

Kirby swung a sardonic sidelong glance her way to query, 'By that, do I take it you mean will we be seeing my parents?'

Her head bobbed up and down quickly. 'Yes.'

'In that case, the answer is no,' he replied curtly. 'Did you think they would be any more enamoured than I was with the way you walked out?'

'No, I suppose not,' she murmured miserably. She had liked Greg and Lenore Whitman and was sorry to have disappointed them.

The morning wore on and, bypassing Townsville around lunchtime, they made towards Tully—the town whose main claim to fame lay in the fact that it recorded the highest annual rainfall of any town in Australia with one hundred and seventy-nine inches being average and three hundred and eleven inches the maximum—then, shortly afterwards, they were skirting Cairns and Kirby was beginning the descent over Roslyndale and bringing them down on to Maiyatta soil.

Joe Gordon, Kirby's stockman and Melanie's father, was there to meet them with a Land Rover and Alix greeted him diffidently, her trepidation growing uncontrollably now that they had actually arrived.

'Alix,' he nodded taciturnly in response, and went on to speak to Kirby.

A rueful smile touched her lips lightly and then was gone. Joe had never been what one would call talkative, so she supposed that where he was concerned at least, his acceptance of her presence had been normal.

On the ride to the house Alix looked about her with interest. A great many changes had taken place since she left and she was quick to notice them. More paddocks had been cleared, burnt, and sown to suitable tropical pasture for his Brahmin cattle and, as they neared the house, she could see there were many more acres under sugar-cane than there had been before. Some had already been burnt and cut, reminding her that the crushing season would be well under way at this time of year, and some were obviously still waiting for the mechanical harvesters to reap the sweet harvest.

Driving between two fields of the towering green grass they came upon the house suddenly and Alix was surprised in this instance to see that, as opposed to the rest of Maiyatta, there had been little change wrought to Kirby's home. It stood on a slight knoll beside the river, set high above the ground on stilts—as was common with most houses in Queensland in order to allow a cooling passage of air underneath—a wide shaded verandah running the length of its front, tall waving palms sited decoratively on either side of the steps.

As Joe began carrying the luggage inside Kirby looked satirically across to Alix. 'Well, do I say, "Welcome home, darling," and carry you up the steps, as before, or would you prefer to make the effort yourself?'

On noting a tall, brown-haired girl walk out on to the verandah to gaze down at them stonily, Alix was very tempted to agree to his former suggestion, but she eventually decided on the latter with a shrug.

'I wouldn't want to get you into any more trouble,' she taunted, her eyes sliding meaningfully to the waiting figure at the top of the steps. 'So perhaps I'd better ...'

Her words halted abruptly as Kirby took her completely unawares and swept her into his arms, pinning her tightly to his hard chest. 'No woman gets me into trouble!' she was informed in a menacing undertone. 'On my property I do as I damned well please.'

'Poor Melly,' Alix succumbed to the temptation to sympathise mockingly as he started on the somewhat steep ascent, and might have added more except that his constricting arms were just about crushing the life out of her. Nevertheless, when her eyes came level with cold brown ones she couldn't resist smiling sweetly at the other girl and exclaiming, 'Good afternoon, Melly! How nice to see you again. Do forgive me for greeting you like this, but Kirby just wouldn't let me attempt the steps on my own. I've been very ill, you know.'

'So I heard,' came the uninterested reply, with no sign of an attempt at friendliness, before reproachful eyes were turned in another direction. 'Kirby, why didn't you tell me . . .'

'I'm sorry, Melanie, I'll be with you in a minute,' he apologised, cutting off what she had been about to say, and apparently forgetting they were on a level footing now as he carried Alix past her into the house.

'Kirby!'

The plaintive wail followed them down the hall and, stretching upwards to look back over his shoulder, Alix grinned to herself and made a faintly censuring sound at the back of her throat.

'Oh, that really did it,' she chided with false concern. 'She's well and truly ready to carve you up now.'

Still bearing his burden without effort, Kirby turned into a bedroom and waited patiently until Joe had deposited her luggage on the floor and then departed. As soon as they were on their own, however, his demeanour changed considerably and with two quick strides he had dumped Alix unceremoniously on the bed and was leaning over her in a threatening manner.

'I feel like doing some carving up myself at present, so don't crowd me too much, Alix, or I just might take you up on that raincheck you offered me at the hospital,' he blazed.

Alix didn't know why she should suddenly feel so unconcerned by his warning, but the feeling was there all the same. Perhaps because she had just seen Melanie ignored for once. Now, with a faintly goading smile she waved an admonishing finger in front of his furious features.

'Oh, but you wouldn't,' she breathed softly. 'You said yourself I might break, remember?'

With the swiftness of a striking snake her wrist was imprisoned by steely fingers and his eyes stared into hers remorselessly. 'Don't try flirting with me, Alix!' he exhorted violently. 'Living in my house puts you in such a vulnerable position it could prove very rash if you went so far with your needling as to forget that you *do* still happen to be my wife!'

The look in his irate blue eyes had Alix biting at her lip and all her new-found confidence deserting her.

'I wasn't f-flirting!' she denied hotly, her cheeks

reddening under his steady gaze. 'I mean, we both know our marriage is a thing of the past, so why would I want to do anything so inadvisable?'

'Maybe because you mistakenly thought you could disrupt all our lives again without reprisal!'

'That's not true! I was only ...' Alix shook her head wearily and turned her face away. He wouldn't appreciate the truth and she was too dispirited to lie. 'Oh, what does it matter?' she said tonelessly. 'I just hadn't realised I was to be seen as little as possible and heard not at all while I was here. Perhaps it would be easier if you gave me a list stating exactly what you do expect of me.'

If possible, Kirby's grip on her wrist tightened. 'You can stop exaggerating for a start! No one's even hinted that's how you should behave.'

'No, but it's what you would prefer, isn't it, Kirby?' She stared upwards with bitter eyes.

'And since when have you ever cared what I preferred?' he demanded with just as much acrimony as he contemptuously released his hold on her. 'All I can remember you caring about was Alix Whitman, so don't expect me to be too considerate of your feelings now. As far as I'm concerned yesterday's love is dead and buried!'

'Off with the old and on with the new, eh?' she made herself quip flippantly.

'It seems an admirable policy.' He started for the door.

'Then perhaps you'd better start considering a divorce!'

He jerked to a stop as if he had been hit by a bullet. 'Don't worry, it's on the agenda,' he grated and kept walking.

So her marriage was to come to an end after all. Alix had begun to think Kirby didn't intend to have their separation made legal, but now that he had told her differently she wasn't quite sure whether she ought to be happy or sad. In some ways she had found it convenient to be married—like when warding off unwanted admirers—but it had also served to continually remind her of a period of extreme disillusionment in her life, and that recollection she would gladly have put far behind her. Oh, well, she sighed and shrugged her thin shoulders, there wasn't much she could do about it either way. It was out of her hands completely now. If he sued for divorce she would just have to go along with it.

But no matter how casually she tried to dismiss the thought as she busied herself unpacking, it still stayed annoyingly close to the surface of her subconscious for the rest of the afternoon, with the result that when she looked up to discover Melanie eyeing her hostilely from the open doorway she was in no frame of mind to be polite to the person she blamed most for the breakdown of her marriage.

'Yes, did you want something, Melly?' she asked deliberately. Melanie hated having her name shortened. 'Something apart from my husband, that is?'

'I'll have him too, you mark my words,' the older girl sneered as she sauntered into the room as if she owned it. 'You might think you've got him back again because he feels sorry for you at the moment—I can see why too, you look a mess!—but you won't be able to keep him. He intends getting a divorce, you know.'

'Does he now?' Alix purposefully kept her voice light as she carried on putting her clothes away. If Melanie had thought to shock her she hadn't succeeded. 'Well, I've got news for you—I couldn't care less! He's all yours ... *if* you can land him,' she smiled implicitly over her shoulder.

'Oh, I can do that all right.'

Her confidence was almost suffocating and Alix determined to sow a few seeds of doubt. 'I wouldn't be too sure, if I were you,' she advised slyly. 'There's many a slip 'twixt cup and lip, as the saying goes.'

'Meaning?'

'Well ...' Alix paused and then smiled aggravatingly. 'It's taken Kirby four years to decide he wants a divorce. If he takes that long again before deciding he wants to marry you, you'll be how old, thirty-two? Mmm, getting on a bit, wouldn't you say?'

'My age has nothing to do with it,' Melanie retorted with a decided bite in her tone. 'In fact, I should think it would be an advantage. As you'll recall, he tried marrying an adolescent and that was a total disaster.'

'Quite true,' Alix had no choice but to agree. 'But unfortunately you're forgetting to allow for personal preference.'

'Personal preference?' Melanie was openly sceptical.

'Mmm, didn't you know?' Alix opened her eyes innocently wide. 'He told me once that he would never consider marrying a woman over thirty because he thought they were far too set in their ways,' she lied blatantly.

'In that case, I have nothing to worry about.' It was Melanie's turn to gloat. 'I'm still only twenty-eight.'

'Ah, yes . . . *now*! But he isn't divorced yet, is he?'

'A mere formality,' Melanie brushed aside that barrier contemptuously. 'They only take a couple of months to be finalised these days.'

Alix took a deep breath before allowing, 'Provided they're not contested.'

'And what grounds would you have for contesting it?' Melanie snorted disdainfully. 'You're the one who did the deserting.'

'But only because it was forced on me,' Alix returned with a sadness which wasn't altogether faked. 'In my counter-suit I shall claim it was due to my husband's adultery—naming you as co-respondent, of course—and you can imagine how long it will take for the courts to clear that messy little lot up, can't you?'

'Why, you miserable little bitch! You don't want him yourself, but you're too dog-in-the-manger to let anyone else have him!'

'Something you should have considered, perhaps, before crowing how easy it would be for you to catch him?' Alix suggested enquiringly. 'It seems it might not be such a picnic for you, after all, doesn't it, Melly?'

'It won't be for you either after I get through telling Kirby about this,' the older girl hissed. 'Just what do you think his reaction will be when he hears what you've had to say?'

Alix swallowed heavily. He would probably slit her throat! Aloud, she replied as nonchalantly as circumstances would allow, 'There's not much he *can* do. I'm as entitled to file a counter-suit as he is to sue for divorce.'

'We'll see about that, we'll just see about *that*!' Melanie threatened, sweeping towards the door. 'You might not be feeling quite so satisfied with yourself once Kirby's finished with you tonight, though.'

A more than distinct probability, Alix was to concede disconsolately when Melanie had gone. But having made her decision—admittedly, an impromptu one—she would follow it through to her utmost. Maybe it was niggardly of her not to allow Kirby's suit to go through uncontested, but why should she make it easier for them? They certainly hadn't taken pity on her four years ago.

Alix dressed with even more care that evening than she had the night before, taking her time before deciding on a becomingly simple dress in blue and white polyester and white cork-heeled sandals. Her make-up was applied extremely carefully and her hair brushed forward slightly at the sides so that it curled comfortingly about her cheeks. She suspected she would need all the comfort she could get in order to see this particular evening through!

The sun had disappeared long ago and the purpling sky had turned to ebony before she could pluck up enough courage to head for the dining room. An aperitif she had willingly forsaken in her bid to gain more time before facing Kirby's anticipated wrath. It was one thing to outface Melanie, but something else again to attempt the same with her husband.

Kirby was still in the sitting room when she arrived, his back to the door as he stared out of the window at the indifferently kept gardens below, a half-filled glass in his hand. Hesitating, Alix took a deep breath, then walked in.

On hearing her footsteps on the polished floor, Kirby swung to face her, his eyes smouldering. 'You took your time,' he accused tersely. 'Clara waited as long as she could to see you, but she does have a family of her own to look after too, you know.'

'I—I'm sorry, I didn't realise she would be waiting,' Alix apologised, watching nervously as he drained his whisky in one mouthful and guessing that it hadn't been his first drink for the evening. 'Shall—shall I collect the food from the kitchen now?'

Kirby deposited his glass on a drink stand beside the large stereo unit, the corners of his mouth pulling down sardonically. 'It won't walk in by itself.'

Alix pressed her lips together but forbore to retaliate. Instead, she spun on her heel and walked through the connecting dining room door to the kitchen where Clara had left their meal prepared and waiting. Before returning with their first course, however, she halted and ran her eyes round the room consideringly. At least this was consistent with the improvements she had noticed outside. It had been somewhat cramped before, if she remembered correctly, but now it was a space-saver's dream. Everything had its own little niche and all the equipment was new.

'Are you planning on eating in there?'

Kirby's rather sarcastic remark brought Alix back to necessities with a wry grimace and she hurried back to the dining room.

'I'm sorry, I was just having a look,' she explained, placing his prawn cocktail before him and then taking a seat at the opposite end of the table. 'You've had the kitchen remodelled.'

'So?'

It didn't augur well for an enjoyable evening, but Alix tried not to be deterred. 'You've hardly touched the rest of the house,' she continued doggedly.

'As I'm hardly ever here, it didn't seem necessary.' Blue eyes surveyed the room slowly as if seeing it for the first time in a long while. 'It's adequate,' he shrugged impassively.

Alix was surprised Melanie hadn't persuaded him into making changes to its, as he had said, adequate, but sombre décor. Tonight was hardly an auspicious time for her to be bringing that girl's name to the fore, though, so she kept silent, eating only a little of the food in front of her because she was too aware that his temper was riding a very fine line. A move in the wrong direction and she was positive all hell would break loose!

Back in the kitchen once more a while later, it merely took her a few minutes to cook their steaks in the microwave oven and serve them together with the tropical salad Clara had left in the fridge, but on returning to the dining room she found to her dismay that Kirby was already three-quarters of the way through another glass of whisky.

'Would you care for a glass of wine?' he asked tautly as she arranged the separate plates and bowls on the table.

'N-no, thank you,' she shook her head quickly. The thought that he might join her was sufficiently discouraging. She wasn't sure how wine mixed with spirits, but when it was combined with the mood he was in tonight the blending could be explosive.

'Nothing worth toasting?' His brows arched insinuatingly.

Alix held her breath and stared helplessly down the length of the table. 'I just don't feel like it, thank you,' she murmured as conciliatorily as possible. 'I—I never was much of a drinker.'

With his own glass halfway to his lips Kirby sent her a narrowed gaze over its rim. 'Is that an indirect way of telling me you think I've had enough?'

'No, of course not!' Alix's patent dismay was genuine. Criticism was the last thing she had meant to imply. In an effort to distract his attention, she leant forward to grasp the first bowl she could lay her hands on, stammering, 'Here, have some—er—asparagus with your steak. It—it's delicious.'

'Don't change the subject, Alix!' He refused the proffered bowl with a sharp movement of his head. 'Your eyes are most expressive. They condemn me every time I take another mouthful.'

'Well, I'm sorry, I didn't intend to,' she whispered huskily, her fingers twining agitatedly in her lap. 'It's nothing to do with me how much you care to drink.'

'How right you are,' he mocked, and deliberately emptied his glass. 'You happily relinquished all your rights where I was concerned some time ago, didn't you?'

She nodded imperceptibly, her throat tight with tension.

'But you're not going to let a little thing like that stop you when there's a chance to cause an upset, though, are you, my love?' he gibed contemptuously, and when Alix didn't reply, repeated with heavy emphasis, '*Are you, my love?*'

Alix still didn't answer, couldn't answer, and he continued in a savagely grating tone, 'So you're going to charge me with adultery, are you? Well, let me tell you something, you vindictive little troublemaker,' he pushed violently out of his chair to lean menacingly over the table. 'You're going to have a bloody hard time proving what you say, because you haven't got a single shred of evidence to verify it! Any lawyer worth his salt would have a flimsy case like yours laughed out of court. So tell me, how confident are you *now* of delaying my plans?'

The ragged pounding of her heart held Alix pinned to her chair as if hypnotised. She had thought herself prepared for this confrontation, but she now knew it had only been a delusion. She was out of answers and her nerves were shot to pieces. Never had she seen Kirby so frighteningly infuriated, and her defences traitorously dissolved like ice beneath the heat of his anger. Nonetheless, it was obvious he expected some sort of reply and she attempted one shakily.

'You knew h-how I felt about you and—and ...' she refused to say the name, 'so I—I think it's only f-fair....'

'*Fair!* What would you know about being fair?' he cut in derisively and, her trance broken, Alix jumped to her feet with a strangled exclamation and rushed for the door.

Kirby was faster than she was, however, and before she could dart through the opening a hand had spun her around to confine her against the wall panelling and strong fingers threaded roughly through her hair.

'It's all in the interests of fairness, is it, Alix?' he jeered as he twisted punishingly the blonde strands caught around his hand. 'But there was no thought of justice when I mentioned it earlier this afternoon, was there? In fact, you were the one who brought the matter up in the first place!' Again he tugged cruelly to ensure she couldn't turn away, bringing unbidden tears to her eyes with the pain. 'No, it's just to spite

Melanie, because you've never liked her and you've been jealous of her since the day you arrived!'

'Me? Jealous of that—that scheming slut! Oh, God, how could you even think such a thing, let alone believe it?' Alix choked incredulously, and tried to put up a hand to shield her eyes from the burning glare of the light overhead. When it encountered the restricting barrier of his arm she hit out at him wildly, crying, 'Let go of me, Kirby, you're ... you're ...' before her voice faded away and she slumped lifelessly into his arms.

When she came to she opened her eyes slowly, frowningly, to find herself lying on a sofa in the sitting room with a cushion beneath her head and Kirby sitting watchfully close beside her.

'Did I faint?' she puzzled weakly.

'Yes.' It was clipped out along with a sharp breath.

'Oh!' She stared up at him in surprise. 'I've never done that before.'

His lips firmed but he didn't say anything until he had reached for a glass from a nearby table, and then it was only to advise, 'Drink this, it will make you feel better.'

Glancing at the golden brown liquid, Alix shook her head gently. 'I'd rather have water, if you don't mind.'

'For heaven's sake, Alix, just drink it, will you? One shot of brandy isn't going to do you any harm,' he sighed.

'I'm sorry,' she mumbled, levering herself up on the

cushion and doing as he suggested. She was too relieved to see his previous fury had abated to want to start another fight by refusing. When she had finished she handed the glass back and swung her legs to the floor carefully to avoid touching him.

His expression unreadable, Kirby proceeded to roll the empty piece of crystal between his hands. 'Go to bed, Alix,' he ordered peremptorily. 'I apologise for forgetting you've only just come out of hospital, but you unfortunately have the power to rile me so much at times I could quite easily throttle you!'

Alix tentatively put out a placatory hand, but she wasn't given an opportunity to speak before he had rounded on her, his eyes blazing like twin fires.

'Damn you, Alix, I told you to get out of here! Believe me, my feelings haven't subsided any—I'm just exerting a little more self-control at the moment—but I can't guarantee how long it will stay that way!' his voice crackled dangerously.

Another warning wasn't necessary and Alix was swiftly on her feet. At the door she spared a hasty glance backwards, but he had resumed his moody contemplation of the glass, his head downbent, and she continued on her way. She was almost to her bedroom when she heard a loud report, followed by the sound of splintering glass, and she thankfully slipped inside and closed the door. It appeared her inoffensive brandy container had suffered the punishment he would have preferred dealing her!

CHAPTER FOUR

Two days later Alix awoke with a decision made. She wasn't going to hang around the house and put up with another day like yesterday! Kirby had been unbearable. He had alternated between bouts of sarcasm and taciturnity until she hadn't known which to expect next, and Melanie had been too irritatingly triumphant to bear. Surprisingly, the only one who had had a few kindly words for her had been the eternally busy Clara, and she had clucked in a motherly fashion about Alix taking a long time to recuperate if she didn't eat more than she had the night before. Of course, Alix hadn't elaborated as to why her meal had hardly been touched, she would rather have Melanie's mother believe it had been caused by a lack of appetite due to her illness than the true reason.

From now on, however, she vowed things would be different. If no one else at Maiyatta had either the time or the inclination to speak to her amiably then she intended taking herself out from under their feet and finding others who would.

At breakfast she broached the subject to Kirby, enquiring casually, 'Would you mind if I took the car today?'

An intent stare travelled the length of the table. 'Why? Were you planning on going somewhere?'

'Yes ... yes, I was as a matter of fact,' she acknowledged coolly. 'I thought I might drive over to Roslyndale and do some shopping.'

'I see.' He shrugged and went on eating for a few seconds, then, 'You still have that cheque I gave you?'

Alix nodded. She didn't intend using it, but she did still have it.

'What time do you expect to be back?'

She waved one hand vaguely. 'Oh, I don't know, some time early this afternoon, I suppose. I'll tell Clara not to bother making any lunch for me before I leave.'

'Okay,' he agreed indifferently. 'The keys are already in it and the tank's full. Just watch how you drive, hmm?'

'Of course. I wouldn't like to think what my reception would be if I happened to put a dent or two in it,' she retorted a trifle tartly.

'That wasn't what I was meaning!'

'Oh!' She looked amazed that he should care what happened to her, and sounded even more so. 'Well, in that case, there's no need to worry because I certainly don't intend going into a hospital again for a long, long time. These last few weeks were enough to last me a lifetime.'

As soon as the meal was concluded Alix returned to her room to collect her bag and, on impulse, threw a towel and a bikini into her carryall. Roslyndale was on the coast and it was certainly hot enough for a swim. She could buy some sandwiches and a drink in town and then take them down to the beach to eat. It would be more enjoyable than sitting in a café or a coffee lounge.

Kirby's car wasn't one she had driven before, but as it was automatic it didn't create any problems, his last car hadn't been a manual either. The road was sealed all the way to town now too, she discovered, and as she cruised along she could see that that wasn't the only thing in the district which had altered. In selected areas the impenetrable rain forest had given way to civilisation. Cane and cattle were the predominant features of the countryside now and she was often called upon to pull over to allow the huge, and heavily laden, cane trailers through on their way to the mill.

With the increasing prosperity of the surrounding farmlands, Roslyndale had changed too. It was much larger now and specialist shops were beginning to expand the town and take over from the general stores. It was also a lot more difficult to find a parking space, Alix discovered ruefully, and it wasn't until she had driven around the main shopping area a few times that she could find a convenient one which had been vacated.

Her first stop was at the bank to cash one of her own cheques and then she made her way slowly down the main street, window-shopping as she went. By the time an empty feeling in her stomach reminded her she needed food, she had purchased two new dresses, another pair of lightweight slacks, a large bottle of spray cologne, and an assortment of inconsequential sundries.

Dabbing with a hankie at the beads of perspiration which were collecting at her temples, Alix looked about her for the nearest take-away food bar and headed quickly towards it. She felt hot, sticky, and tired, and the promise of the refreshing swim which was shortly to come was the only thing keeping her going. The few hours spent walking had sapped her small reserves of strength and she was more than ready for a rest.

She gave her order to a fresh-faced teenager behind the counter and waited for it to be filled while gratefully standing beneath the whirring blades of a ceiling fan, gradually becoming aware of a laughing couple next to her, the girl seeming somehow familiar. It wasn't until they had all finished paying for their cartons of food and had walked out on to the pavement that she could recall her name, though.

Almost at the same time, the dark-haired girl put out a hesitant hand to touch Alix on the arm and query, 'Excuse me, but aren't you Alix Whitman?'

A confirming smile and Alix exclaimed, 'And you're Karen Aylward! I thought I recognised you in the shop, but I wasn't quite sure. You've changed considerably.' Karen had only been sixteen when she had first met her.

'So have you,' Karen laughed. 'I can always remember thinking what an unfair difference two years made. At sixteen I was still being treated like a schoolkid, while at eighteen, you were already married.' The young man with her cleared his throat meaningfully and she grinned. 'Oh, I'm sorry, you never met my brother Tim, did you? As I recollect, he was away contracting with his trucks when you were here before.'

'My misfortune,' the husky blond giant next to her smiled. 'Nice to meet you, Alix. Are you back for good now?'

She shook her head wryly. 'No, only until I've recovered from an annoying attack of pneumonia.'

'Then you and Kirby haven't . . .' Karen began, and then flushed with embarrassment. 'I'm sorry, I shouldn't have said that, it's none of my business. Shall we talk about something else?'

'No, that's all right,' Alix shrugged. 'Everyone knows Kirby and I separated, so I guess it's only reasonable to expect a few raised eyebrows when people realise I'm back again. But I'm here for my health, that's all, nothing else has changed.' Except, of course, that soon they would be divorced and not just separated!

'And judging by what you've just bought, about to eat lunch,' Tim inserted smoothly, easing the atmosphere. 'Where were you intending to have it? On the way home, or here in town?'

'On the beach, actually,' Alix smiled gratefully at

him. Although she might outwardly pretend it didn't worry her talking about her marriage, inwardly it was a different story. 'I've been looking forward to it for the last hour or more.'

'Great minds think alike, then, because that's where we're headed,' Karen relayed cheerily. 'How about we join forces?'

Alix nodded pleasurably. 'I'd like that.'

It was decided they would make for palm-fringed Sandspit Bay and after thankfully depositing her parcels on the back seat of the car it didn't take Alix long to drive the mile or so out of town and park on the grassy edge of the dunes. Karen was spreading a rug in the shade provided by the trees when she arrived and Tim had already changed into sky blue swimming shorts in order to offer a darkly tanned back to the sun.

'Come and sit down,' Karen invited. 'I thought we could pool our resources and make a picnic of it. How does that sound to you?'

'Fine,' Alix grinned as she sank down on to the rug and laid out her purchases. 'I've got corned beef and tomato, curried egg and tuna, an apple, and a can of pineapple juice.'

'And we've got chicken, ham salad, steak and tomato, two bananas, two oranges, a can of lime and a can of cola. Now, how's that for a goodly selection?' Karen laughed, sitting back on her heels.

'All very well if you're just going to sit there and list them,' put in Tim drily. 'But how about we start disposing of it, hmm? I'm starving!'

She pulled a laughing grimace and passed him a triangle of steak and tomato. 'Oh, here, make your miserable life happy,' she teased. 'But I warn you, we're staying for that swim afterwards. You're not rushing me off immediately we've finished.'

'Uh-uh, it's too late for that,' he grinned lazily. 'We may as well make a day of it now we're here.'

For Alix's benefit, Karen explained, 'He didn't want to be in town too long this morning because they're so busy hauling cane at the moment, but the time sort of got away from me while I was searching for a new evening gown.' She glanced across to her brother with a bantering look. 'It's lucky we always have spare costumes in the car, but I noticed he didn't exactly shout me down when I suggested lunch on the beach and a quick swim though.'

'I wasn't game,' he retorted. 'You would have made my life hell all the way home if I had.'

Although there was quite a disparity in their ages— Alix guessed that Tim would have been closer to thirty, if not past it, rather than Karen's twenty—it was obvious they shared a very close relationship. But she also thought she could remember there being other children in the family and she mentioned this to Karen.

'Oh, yes, there's more of us,' the other girl laughed ruefully. 'Simon, David, and Peter, to be exact—and all older than me. They're partners with Tim in the cane trucks.'

Alix nodded thoughtfully, it was coming back to her now, but the eldest of Karen's brothers had more to impart on the subject and his grey eyes were twinkling as he leant across for another sandwich.

'Mmm, the folks gave up in disgust when this one came along, she was such a disappointment.'

'Hah!' Karen snorted disparagingly. 'If I'd been the first born they wouldn't have bothered with the four of you.'

'Probably not,' he agreed, to Alix's surprise, then added, 'But only because, as I said, their disappointment would have been so great.'

Their lighthearted camaraderie was a balm to Alix's torn emotional state and as they weren't averse to drawing her into their bantering conversation she felt more relaxed and carefree than she had done for a long while by the time their lunch was finally finished.

'And you and your brothers own all those can haulers I saw on my way in to town, do you, Tim?' Alix asked as they rested, replete, after their meal.

'Those servicing the Roslyndale mill, we do,' he qualified.

'And the trucks are filled with chopped cane by the harvesters, are they?'

'No, they have what are called field buggies for that,' he explained willingly. 'They carry about a seven tonne load which is then tipped into one of a number of twenty tonne steel bins which are on loading pads nearby. Once the bins are filled they're then winched on to semi-trailers and driven to the mill where they're winched off again. An empty bin is then collected, returned to a loading pad, and the next full bin is loaded back on again. And so it goes on, and on ...'

'Until the season is finished, I suppose,' she smiled. 'Then what?'

He grinned cheerfully. 'Then we head south and carry vegetable crops from farms to the canneries. The two work in quite well.'

'And just how long does the cane crushing season last?' When she had been in the area last time she hadn't stayed long enough to find out, she remembered wryly.

'The mills are usually in operation between June and December each year, but sometimes it spills over into January if there's too much rain in the summer months and it stops the harvesters from working,' he said, and then eyed her enquiringly as he asked, 'Would you like to see over the mill?'

'Very much,' she nodded, her interest aroused. 'But are the public allowed in?'

'They are when their husband's a part owner,' he laughed. 'Seriously though, and all jokes aside, yes the public are allowed in. In fact, most mills have become so used to visitors asking for guided tours that all you have to do now is to follow the yellow arrows marked on the floor and you can take yourself around any time you wish. They do still give guided tours, of course, for school children and the like, but in most cases they've found people would prefer to view it at their leisure rather than be held to a particular time. So, nowadays, you just present yourself at the main office where they'll give you a map of the mill and all kinds of literature on sugar—which cover from planting to refining—and as you follow the marked course you'll find boards up at the relevant places of interest with diagrams showing what's happening, together with all the explanatory notes you're ever likely to need.'

'Well, for heaven's sake, is it really as easy as all that?' Alix asked, astonished, but before giving him time to reply had gone on to questions, 'And Kirby is a part owner of the Roslyndale mill, is he?'

Although Karen looked somewhat taken aback by Alix having to ask others regarding her husband's interests, Tim's expression wasn't quite so obvious and he replied unhesitatingly.

'Sure is. All the cane-growers round here are part owners. It's run as a co-operative, like a large percentage of the sugar mills are. They own it, manage it, and share in the profits ... or losses.'

'I see,' Alix pursed her lips meditatively.

She hadn't realised before just how ignorant she was of Kirby's life, and his *way* of life, and she was finding the perception peculiarly unsettling. So much so that when Karen suggested the pair of them should change into their swimming costumes too so they could sample the delights of the Coral Sea a few yards distant, she accepted with an alacrity out of all proportion to that which was required.

They used their cars as changing rooms and it didn't take either of them long to exchange their sundresses for bikinis, although when she emerged into the sunlight again Alix was very aware of the startling contrast between Karen and Tim's bronzed skins and her own winter paleness. Gratefully, she discovered the difference wasn't so noticeable when they were in the warm blue water and after they had spent the best part of an hour swimming lazily and diving for shells, her selfconsciousness had all but disappeared.

'That was lovely,' she sighed contentedly a while later as they spread out their towels on the hot sand. 'I shall have to do this more often while I'm here, it's ages since I've been swimming.'

'Well, if you have nothing planned for the day after tomorrow I'd be pleased to escort you around the mill in the morning and drive you down here for a picnic afterwards,' Tim offered amiably.

'Oh, but I couldn't let you do that,' Alix protested. 'I know you must be terribly busy now that the season's in full swing.'

'He's not *that* busy,' chipped in Karen subtly.

'No, I think the business can survive without me supervising it for every hour of each day,' he confirmed wryly.

'Well, in that case ...' Alix sifted a handful of sand between her fingers indecisively before asking, 'You're sure?'

Karen grinned broadly. 'Of course he's sure. Tim

'Well, of course I did, but I only meant it as a general guide,' she grimaced. 'I didn't know you were going to use it as a curfew!'

'I wasn't, damn you, but I dislike intensely having to ring all over town in a futile attempt to discover my own wife's whereabouts!'

So his pride had been hurt, had it? she mused speculatively. Well, that made it one point in her favour.

'If you must know,' she smiled, not a little smugly, 'I've been to the beach. Can't you tell?' as she waved a decidedly pink-tinged arm under his nose.

Kirby's features hardened but he didn't move as he mocked bitingly, 'And it was such fun you couldn't tear yourself away until it was dark, I suppose?'

'Spot on!' Alix facetiously gave him a thumbs-up sign and went to walk past him.

This time he moved, quickly and deliberately, and her arm felt as if it was being broken as it was caught in an iron grip and she was hauled intimidatingly close to his powerful frame.

'Don't give me any of your cute answers, you aggravating little so-and-so!' he blazed down at her wrathfully. 'I want to know where you've been and I mean to find out *now*!'

At his persistent questioning Alix's own temper was beginning to get the better of her and she flared back immediately. 'As I told you, I was at the beach ... with *friends*!' she emphasised caustically. 'You know, those people the dictionary describes as being ones who are *easy* to get on with!'

He ignored the pointed sarcasm and went right to the heart of the matter. 'What friends? You never bothered to make any while you were here!'

'Well, I obviously have now, haven't I?' she taunted. But by the look that came into his metallic blue eyes Alix knew it just as obviously hadn't been the right type of retaliation to make and she moderated it grudgingly. 'Okay, okay, so I was with Karen and Tim Aylward. Does that make you feel any better?'

'Not particularly,' he snapped. 'Should it?'

'Well, they're friends of yours too, aren't they?'

'And just because Tim happens to be a friend of mine, you think I ought to be pleased to know my wife's in the company of another man, do you?'

'I don't see why not!' she returned heatedly. All this fuss because of a slightly damaged ego! 'At least he's willing to take some time off from his work to be sociable, *and* he's offered to take me over the mill, which is a hell of a lot more than you ever did!'

'That's hardly surprising!' Kirby bit out acidly. 'You never showed the slightest interest in it before.'

Alix's shoulders drooped tiredly. She couldn't honestly deny the truth of his statement. 'Perhaps you never gave me a reason to,' she murmured, depressed.

The taut silence which followed her dejected accusation stretched her nerves almost to breaking point and it was with a shuddering sigh of relief that she felt Kirby slowly release his hold on her.

'You could be right,' he conceded heavily, and causing her eyes to fly to his in amazement. 'You didn't really get a fair go, did you?'

It was the closest he had ever come to apologising for the lack of time he had spent with her and suddenly tears for what they had lost welled into her wide-spaced eyes which she had to blink away swiftly. It was too little, too late, she cried sadly to herself.

To Kirby she gave a tremulous half smile and owned candidly, 'I didn't exactly give you one either.'

His answering smile was an ironic agreement, but the increase in Alix's rapid breathing had nothing whatsoever to do with their discussion, it was purely an involuntary reaction to the quality of his physical appeal. When he looked at her like that he had always been able to raise her pulse rate and, in an effort to camouflage the effect he was having on her equilibrium, she hurried into defensive speech.

'Oh, well, I guess it's all history now. We'll just have to chalk it up to experience, won't we?' she advocated with forced brightness.

'In order to avoid the same pitfalls next time?'

'I s-suppose so,' she faltered. For her there definitely wouldn't be a next time but, of course, she had forgotten he was contemplating taking another plunge into the sea of matrimony. An oddly disturbing recollection.

Alix had watched the trim and efficient Clara Gordon darting busily around the house all the following morning and by afternoon she thought it was time to speak up. She had done absolutely nothing all day and she was bored to tears.

'Clara, isn't there something, *anything*, I can do to save you some time?' she queried plaintively as the woman rushed back into the kitchen for the second time to check on her baking.

'You mean, you *want* to do something?' Clara turned away from the oven with her hazel eyes widening.

'Well, of—of course.' Alix looked startled herself now. 'I used to want to help before but . . .' she lifted one shoulder embarrassedly, 'I didn't quite know how to mention it. You were always so super-competent I thought you might take offence if I said I wanted to take a hand, so I ended up not saying anything at all.'

'Oh, my goodness!' Clara sank down on to a bright red kitchen stool, one hand spread over her chest. 'And I thought it was because you were too haughty to be interested.'

'Heavens, no! I would have loved something to do.' To keep her mind off Kirby's absence, if for no other reason.

'Well, if you really want to,' Clara began slowly, as if still a little unsure she had heard correctly, 'you could take over the preparation of the meals for me— that would be a great help. Although,' her forehead creased doubtfully, 'Kirby may have something to say about it. Don't forget, you are only supposed to be resting.'

'Right at the moment I feel that if I rest any more I

shall probably fall into a compulsive hibernation and never wake up again,' Alix protested drily. 'I really do feel much stronger, Clara, and I'm sure I'll recover faster if there's something I can occupy myself with.'

'All right, then,' the older woman relented with a smile. 'I was planning on making sweet and sour pork for you tonight, so if you could take over that while keeping an eye on the apricot crumble in the oven to see it doesn't burn, it will help me no end and let me get on with cleaning out the office.'

'As good as done,' Alix laughed, her blue-green eyes shining happily in anticipation. 'You've just gone a long way towards reconciling me to my period of convalescence, Clara.'

'And you've just done a lot to reaffirm my faith in your husband's judgment,' was the totally unexpected reply, and as an explanation in view of Alix's puzzled frown, 'I never could understand how Kirby had been taken in so completely by those cool blonde looks of yours. Now I know that he wasn't!'

It was one of the most touching compliments Alix had ever received, and it was made doubly so considering the source was, of all people, Melanie's mother. But it also conjured up memories and her expression saddened immeasurably.

'Ah, but that was a long time ago, Clara,' she sighed. 'You know he's planning to file for a divorce, don't you?'

'Oh, I don't believe it! He didn't say so, surely?'

Alix was positive the woman's disbelief was genuine, and yet ... Was it really possible she didn't know the part her own daughter had played in their troubles?

'He said, and I quote, "it's on the agenda",' she divulged dully.

'But that's ridiculous! I mean ...' Clara stopped and peered at Alix closely. '*You* don't want a divorce, do you?'

'Now there's a question I should know the answer to straight away—but I don't,' Alix laughed brokenly. 'I used to think I wanted one, but—but ...'

'Having met him again, you're not so sure, hmm?'

'Maybe I'm just being petty,' Alix put forward Melanie's argument wryly. 'I don't want to be married to him, but I don't want anyone else to be either!'

'Rubbish!' Clara dismissed the idea contemptuously. 'If you'd truly got the man out of your system you wouldn't care who was married to him.'

'But I'm not still in love with him—I know I'm not,' was the vigorous denial. She couldn't possibly be! Not after all this time.

'Well, you've got plenty of time in which to find out just how you do feel,' Clara smiled encouragingly. 'One thing's for sure, if he didn't divorce you while you were separated, he certainly won't start proceedings while you're living in his house.'

'Don't you think so?'

'I *know* so,' Clara stated positively as she headed for the door. Then she suddenly turned back, her expression wry. 'But while you're thinking over what I've said, you won't forget to check the oven, will you?'

With a laugh, Alix promised, 'I'll do it now,' and fulfilled it as soon as Clara had gone. The crumble still wasn't quite ready, however, and she left it for a few minutes longer.

In the meantime, as she set about preparing their evening meal her thoughts did, as Clara had intimated they would, keep returning to what had been said. Up until then she had honestly believed her idea to contest the divorce had been brought about solely by Melanie's attitude, but now she wasn't sure if that hadn't just been a convenient cover for a subconscious wish of her own. It was true Kirby still attracted her in a physical sense, but now she had to decide if that's all it was, or if there was some other, deeper, emotion involved as well.

When they sat down to dinner she was still turning it over in her mind and while Kirby was occupied with his food she decided to take the chance to study him critically. Unfortunately, her scheme wasn't very successful because she abruptly found her scrutiny being shrewdly returned and she dropped her gaze to her plate in confusion.

'A penny for them.'

'I'm sorry?' Alix automatically looked up again, her eyes questioning.

'Your thoughts,' he elucidated with a lightly mocking smile which promptly scattered the entire contents of her mind to the four winds.

'They weren't anything important,' she laughed disparagingly. 'I was—er—they were . . .'

'Mmm?'

In desperation she looked frantically about her until her glance came to rest on the french doors. 'I was thinking you needed new curtains,' she dissembled quickly. 'Those ones are—are too heavy. They make the room very dark during the day.'

One corner of his mouth tilted devastatingly. 'That's odd! I don't remember you finding anything wrong with them before.'

Alix stared at him powerlessly. He was deliberately tormenting her and they both knew it. 'Well, I—I do now,' she valiantly tried to hold his taunting gaze. 'Or don't you believe in allowing people to change their minds?'

'That depends on what their thoughts were originally,' he drawled.

Something Alix had no intention of revealing. With a discomfited movement of one shoulder she made as if to rise and end the baiting conversation. 'If you've finished I'll get the dessert,' she offered.

Kirby shook his head negatively. 'I haven't, but more importantly, neither have you. So far you've only finished one complete dinner since you've been here and, at that rate, I can see your return to full health isn't going to be accomplished very rapidly.'

And he would prefer to have her off the place as soon as possible, surmised Alix dolefully.

'Not at all,' Kirby's voice broke in on her reverie, making her wonder if she had spoken her thoughts aloud until he disclosed with a lazy grin, 'Your face, my love, is still as expressive as it ever was. It wasn't difficult to tell what conclusion you'd arrived at after my last comment.'

'Very clever,' she grimaced. There wasn't much use denying it. 'You make me sound as transparent as a sheet of glass.'

'But only of the frosted variety. The outline's there . . . it's just not very clearly defined.'

At least that was something. It would have been intolerable if he had suspected any of her other thoughts. Alix began to eat slowly, thoughtfully.

CHAPTER FIVE

'By the way,' Kirby began at breakfast the next morning, 'I was talking to Tim on the phone earlier and he asked me to give you a message. He's very sorry but, owing to unforeseen circumstances, he won't be able to take you over the mill today after all.'

Alix was immediately suspicious. He sounded inordinately pleased with what he was relaying.

'Oh, I didn't hear the phone when it rang,' she said, deliberately offhand as she began spreading apricot jam on her toast. 'What time was it when he called?'

'He didn't, I rang him.'

Alix dropped her knife on to her plate with a clatter. She really hadn't expected him to admit it so openly. 'In order to tell him you weren't going to allow me to go with him, I suppose?' she fumed.

Kirby disagreed indolently. 'No, I merely suggested that, as I was intending to visit the mill today myself, there was no necessity for him to leave his work since you would be able to come with me instead.'

'You never mentioned anything about going to the mill!' she denounced angrily, glaring at him. 'And how dare you so arbitrarily alter my arrangements! Now you've spoilt everything—we were going to the beach again afterwards too.'

84

'You didn't tell me that.'

'What? That we were going to the beach?' she queried, and then gibed, 'Why should I? I didn't think you'd care where I was as long as I was out of your way.'

'Your second mistake,' he drawled.

'And my first?'

'In thinking I would allow your arrangements with Tim to stand.' His tone hardened fractionally.

'Oh, yes, I was forgetting that fragile male pride of yours, wasn't I?' she taunted, controlling her temper with difficulty.

Kirby inhaled a deep breath and ground out softly, but forcefully, 'Do you want to come or not?'

Of course she did! But she couldn't allow him to dictate her movements without showing some spark of rebellion.

'Yes,' she muttered with ill grace when she felt the silence had been stretched for long enough, but still added for good measure, 'Although I was looking forward to another afternoon at the beach too.'

His mouth curved wryly. 'Is that a hint?'

'Well . . .' She spread her hands wide and sent him an artless look. 'The two were planned as a single outing, and you *were* the one who disrupted the arrangement.'

At first Alix thought he had only been mocking her with his question and that he wasn't going to agree, but then to her astonishment he shook his head and uttered a short disbelieving laugh. 'I'm not quite sure why you should but, okay, you win. You'd better ask Clara if she can pack some lunch for us.'

'I'll do it,' she proposed cheerfully. 'I'm in charge of all meals now.'

'Oh?' He looked at her askance. 'Since when?'

Her aquamarine eyes clouded temporarily. 'Y-yes-terday afternoon,' she stammered, uncertain of his response. 'I need something to do while I'm here and—and last night's dinner wasn't too bad, was it?'

'Most satisfactory,' he acknowledged lazily. 'But I never knew you were so domesticated, my love.'

The thought that he appeared ready to accept the status quo enabled her to answer airily. 'That's only one of my various skills, Kirby, I do assure you.'

'Oh, I can believe that,' he retorted drily. 'It's more than obvious you've changed in a number of ways during the past four years.'

'For better or worse?' she couldn't resist asking.

His ensuing smile had Alix chewing at her lip worriedly. The attraction he held for her was still tremendously strong and she didn't want it to be. She wanted to be able to view the situation objectively and she couldn't do that while her capricious emotions kept getting in the way.

'That's a leading question and I think we would both prefer not hear the answer,' he replied ironically.

'I suppose so,' she smiled, but the strain of doing so made her facial muscles ache. What on earth had possessed her to ask such a question? Of course he didn't think she had improved. Hadn't his attitude already told her that plainly enough?

Alix finished her breakfast quickly and headed for the kitchen with the dishes to stand for a moment with her hands clasping the edge of the sink, her head bent. She was still standing there when Melanie entered the room via the back door.

'Poor Alix,' she pretended commiseration. 'Have you had another defeat at Kirby's hands?'

It was enough to dispel her previous depression and Alix straightened with a taunting laugh. 'No, a success, actually,' she enjoyed informing her antagonist. 'He's taking me out for the day.'

'To watch the cane being burnt?' Melanie scoffed.

'No, to the mill ... and the beach,' sweetly.

The other girl's eyes narrowed spitefully. 'You're lying!' she hissed. 'Why would he take you anywhere?'

'Because he wants to, presumably.'

'In consideration for what? An uncontested divorce?'

'Good lord, no,' Alix laughed, thoroughly pleased with the annoyance she was creating. 'I wouldn't sell out my principles that cheaply, Melly.'

'No, you'd be certain to want everything you could get your hands on! But if that's not the reason he's doing it, what is?' The narrowed eyes glared at her suspiciously.

'Perhaps you should ask Kirby,' Alix suggested. 'I'm sure he'll be thrilled to know you're so interested in his every decision.'

'He knows that already. I help him with most of them,' the brunette mocked.

'But not this one, apparently,' Alix reminded her silkily. 'This time he left you right out in the cold.'

'Not for long, though. He'll be pleased to tell me if I ask him,' was the confident reply.

Alix smiled sardonically, her eyes ranging pointedly over the other girl. 'In that case, let's hope you're as pleased with his reply.'

Melanie slammed out of the kitchen with a furious epithet on her lips and Alix sank down on to the stool with a wry look of disgust. So much for Miss Gordon! She really was the most objectionable female she had ever met and their confrontations drained her both mentally and physically. She might have been more able to meet Melanie on her own footing this time, but that certainly didn't make it any the more pleasant.

With their picnic lunch packed in a cooler chest and having changed into burgundy-coloured slacks and a white cotton top, Alix went looking for her husband not knowing quite what to expect since Melanie would have undoubtedly spoken to him. She met him coming up the steps on to the verandah as she came out through the doorway.

'Are we still going?' she asked uncertainly.

'Is there any reason we shouldn't?'

The counter-question had been coolly made and Alix felt her spirits sink. 'I thought you may have changed your mind,' she disclosed dejectedly.

'Due to any particular cause, or just for the hell of it?' he queried sarcastically.

On a swallowed sob Alix spun away and started back down the hall. So once again Melanie had succeeded in causing dissension between them. Her day out was ruined before it had even begun.

'Alix! Will you come back here?'

Kirby's voice sounded angrily behind her, but with only a violent shake of her head for an answer she kept going until she reached the kitchen. A fraction of a second later he burst into the room impatiently.

'What do you think you're doing?' he questioned on seeing her lift the lid of the chest and start removing items.

'It's obvious, isn't it? I'm putting the picnic things away,' she reported lifelessly, and when he calmly began replacing them all again frowned, 'What are you doing that for?'

'Because we'll be needing them in a few hours' time,' he advised roughly, and catching hold of her wrist in one hand, and the chest in the other, pulled her out of the room after him.

She was thrust in the passenger seat of the car with as little ceremony as she had been hauled through the house and the chest dumped in the back, but when he slid in beside her and went to turn over the engine Alix put out a hand to effectively stop him.

'I'm sorry, Kirby, but I don't think this is such a good idea, after all,' she sighed miserably. 'It's not going to be pleasant for either of us if we're at each other's throats all day.'

The eyes which raked over her despairing face

were bitter. 'Then maybe you should have thought of that before gloating to Melanie how you had at last found a way to make me leave my work in order to escort you around, and that if I wanted an uncontested divorce your price was going to be a high one!' he snapped.

'But I didn't say that!' she protested vehemently. 'She's twisted my words around completely. *She* was the one who suggested you were only being nice to me and taking me out today because you were hoping for an uncontested divorce in return!'

'In payment for one trip to the mill and the beach?' He was openly disbelieving. 'Doesn't that sound a little far-fetched . . . even to you?'

'And that's why I said it wouldn't come so cheaply!' she cried, trying desperately to convince him.

'But—provided the circumstances were suitable— you would be prepared to negotiate, I gather,' he charged scornfully.

'Negotiate?' she repeated in confusion. Just what *had* Melanie said to him? 'I'm—I . . . no, I would not be prepared to negotiate,' she denied stormily.

'Not even for half the value of the property?'

If that was the price Melanie had put on her principles then she had undervalued them by a long way. 'Not even for the whole of it,' she retorted disgustedly.

Kirby exhaled heavily, his taut expression turning rueful. 'I must admit I found it hard to believe you'd become quite so mercenary. I guess Melanie must have misunderstood you.'

'What other reason could there possibly be for such conflicting stories?' Alix questioned caustically, but the sarcasm appeared lost on Kirby, for he merely nodded as if in approval.

The sugar mill was on the other side of Roslyndale and as they drove through the main gate Alix could see two of Tim's semi-trailers about to off-load their overflowing bins of cane. The sight of them reminded her what he had said about visitors to the mill and as they alighted from the car at the office building she turned to Kirby with a deprecatory shrug.

'If you want to conduct your business I can go round by myself,' she volunteered. 'Tim said it was allowed.'

'It's allowed,' he agreed. 'But is that how you would prefer it?'

It didn't take her long to decide. 'No,' she admitted with a somewhat shy smile. 'I'd rather have someone there to explain things as I go along.'

His dark brows peaked teasingly. 'Someone?'

'All right, then ... you,' she laughed, but in case he got the wrong idea, promptly added, 'I don't know anyone else to ask.'

Alix declined his offer to accompany him into the manager's office but took a seat in the foyer and began thumbing through the brochures the receptionist had supplied her with. She had hardly finished the first one before Kirby was back again.

'That didn't take long,' she said, rising to her feet

and walking with him towards the glass doors. 'Couldn't you have said all you wanted to say over the phone? Or ...' she paused and sent him a searching look, 'would that have defeated the purpose?'

Muscular shoulders were flexed dispassionately beneath their slate blue, silk knit covering. 'The personal touch often produces better results,' he declared equably.

Although she strongly suspected his motives, Alix didn't press the matter. If the truth were known she was probably happier to be in her husband's company anyway. At least she had no worries about him wanting an affair just because she was separated!

As they neared the first crushing plant Alix could feel the concrete beneath their feet vibrating with the force of the machinery inside, and her nose was quick to register the permeating, sickly sweet smell which emanated from the building. Her first impression as they entered the open-ended structure was of clouds of steam, pistons, pulleys, conveyors, and *noise*! So much noise that she had to concentrate extremely hard to hear what Kirby was saying as he explained how the cane was weighed and analysed on arrival because payment was made to growers on the sugar content of their crops, not on the quantity of cane delivered.

From a continuous conveyor the cane stalks entered what was called a "shredder" where revolving blades ripped and tore the stalks to pieces so the crushing mills could accept them more readily. There were four sets of rollers the fibre passed through to extract the sugar juice and while this was then fed into a clarifier, the fibre remaining after the final crushing—"bagasse", as Kirby informed her—was used as a fuel in the boiler furnace to provide most of the power and heat required by the factory.

Once the impurities had been extracted and the juice filtered, it then proceeded to the evaporators where it was concentrated by boiling off the water and then boiled again in a vacuum pan until crystals of raw sugar formed. This part of the operation, Kirby advised, had a large bearing on the quality of the sugar as this depended heavily on the size and uniformity of the crystals. As soon as they had reached the correct size, however, they were then released through the bottom of the pan into centrifugals— perforated baskets—which spun at high speed to throw off the surrounding dark syrup—molasses— and the remaining pale brown crystals were then tumble-dried and transferred to bulk storage.

'And it takes seven tonnes of cane to make one tonne of raw sugar,' Alix mused over Kirby's last piece of information as they walked slowly out of the building. Then, with her eyes enquiringly raised, 'But why don't they keep going and refine it straight away? Why leave it in a raw state?'

'Because it can be stored for longer periods in that form and it's also cheaper and more readily transported that way.'

'I see,' she nodded, another question forming. 'And

once it reaches the refinery, what do they do with it?'

If he was tired of her queries Kirby didn't show it and answered informatively, 'Well, raw sugar is comprised of ninety-eight per cent sucrose and two per cent impurities, and the refiners remove that two per cent—which are non-sugar substances—by a process of washing, dissolving, filtering through bone-charcoal to achieve that whiter-than-white look, crystallising, separating and drying, which results in a product that's ninety-nine point nine per cent sucrose and one of the purest foodstuffs manufactured.'

Again Alix nodded. She hadn't realised it was such a long and complicated process. 'And the molasses back there?' She waved a hand towards the mill. 'Is that where treacle and golden syrup originate?'

Kirby smiled and shook his head as he opened the car door for her. 'No, they're a product of refining. Some of the syrup left behind is mixed with different forms of sugar such as fructose and glucose, then concentrated to remove any water and this becomes treacle. Golden syrup is essentially the same product except that it's been lightened in colour by being put through the charcoal filters.'

Alix pulled her perspiration-soaked top away from her back as she waited for Kirby to walk around the car and then wrinkled her nose wryly in the direction of the mill when he resumed his seat beside her.

'I'm surprised you don't charge people for sauna baths,' she grinned. 'I certainly feel as if I've just had one!'

'Mmm, you do look a little wilted around the

edges,' he smiled teasingly, but appearing hardly affected by the steamy conditions himself, Alix noted with disgust. 'Never mind, you'll be able to cool off at the Bay in a short while.'

Well, at least reduce her temperature to some degree, she corrected drily to herself. In north Queensland's tropical waters she had always found it was practically impossible to *cool* off! She supposed it was just a matter of becoming acclimatised, but as her visits had never been of sufficient duration for that adjustment to take place, she was finding even the warmth of winter to be a trifle enervating. The near freezing temperatures she had left behind in Canberra definitely hadn't prepared her for the hot and humid conditions of a sugar mill!

The tide was out when they arrived at the beach, leaving the long curving sandspit which had given the sweeping bight its name exposed to view at the southern end, and after hurriedly changing into their costumes they took the opportunity to walk along it while it was still available.

On either side it shelved gradually into the clear blue-green water which matched Alix's eyes exactly and it was possible to see all manner of marine life scurrying about their business in the light-filled shallows. The south-east trade wind coming off the sea lifted strands of hair gently from Alix's forehead and she turned her face towards it appreciatively. It was the first sign of a breeze she had experienced all morning.

Seeing the gesture, though, Kirby immediately suggested, 'I reckon a swim is called for, how about you?'

'I can hardly wait,' she smiled, albeit a trifle faintly. 'I've noticed the heat even more today than I did when I went shopping.'

'You're sure you feel okay?' he frowned watchfully. 'I hardly think a case of heatstroke would be particularly beneficial in your condition.'

'No, no, I'm not that bad,' Alix dismissed the suggestion ruefully. 'Besides, a symptom of heatstroke is a cessation of sweating, isn't it? and I can assure you I haven't, unfortunately, reached that stage yet.'

His deep, husky laugh at her wry expression had Alix's heart beginning to pound erratically. If only he wasn't so damnably attractive, she despaired, and running back the way they had come to avoid his bright gaze, she plunged beneath the first incoming wave.

A few seconds later Kirby dived cleanly beneath the following breaker and regained his feet on the other side. 'That was quick, wasn't it? One moment you were there and the next you'd gone,' he commented drily.

Alix waded further out to meet the next wave, shrugging as she went. 'I just couldn't wait any longer, it was too tempting,' she half smiled.

The sight of his bronzed torso glistening with jewelled drops of water was suddenly making her feel inexplicably shy and she berated herself for it grimly. For heaven's sake, she had lived intimately with the man for six months, hadn't she? She had certainly seen more of him than she was seeing today! However, she discovered that wasn't a thought likely to help subdue her wayward emotions either and, in defence, she sought to put more distance between them.

A powerful crawl inexorably closed the gap again. 'It's easier by boat, you know,' he drawled.

'What is?' Twin lines of puzzlement creased her forehead.

'To see the Reef,' he smiled ironically. 'I thought you might have been planning to swim all the way out there.'

It was only then that Alix realised she couldn't touch bottom any more and had begun to automatically tread water. 'I—I just prefer deeper water for swimming, that's all,' she offered with staged nonchalance in explanation and, as if to prove her point, started off in a line parallel to the beach.

Her strength wasn't such that it permitted her to swim too far, however, and when she surfaced again it was to see Kirby standing in the same spot she had left him, his arms folded patiently across his chest, his head tilted slightly to one side.

'Which direction are you going to try now?' he taunted.

Without wanting him to guess the reason for her evasive actions, or to appear incredibly childish, Alix knew she had no choice except to swim back again, but she did so in as leisurely fashion as was possible, taking her time and heading for waist deep water so she could stand.

'Aren't you going to swim too?' she made herself ask brightly. 'It's wonderfully relaxing.'

'Is that so?' His well shaped mouth levelled abruptly. 'Then maybe I should, because I sure feel the need for something calming at the moment.'

Alix blinked the water from her eyes and watched him uneasily. She surmised he was annoyed with her behaviour but fighting hard to control it and she didn't want to upset the delicate balance. Kirby's glittering gaze held hers momentarily and then, twisting away with a smothered exclamation Alix couldn't make out, he dived and began cutting through the water with a powerful stroke. Alix didn't know whether to wait where she was or to head for the sand, but when the next wave nudged her shorewards she didn't oppose it, merely letting it carry her as far as it wanted while her troubled eyes remained glued to the dark head making for the northern end of the beach.

Sighing, she left the water and sat on the wet sand, drawing her legs up and resting her chin on her knees as she idly picked out patterns with a piece of driftwood and then watched impassively when the turning tide gently obliterated them.

'You want to watch you don't burn,' Kirby's voice sounded a warning when he returned and began pushing through the shallows towards her. 'You're very pale.'

'I know,' she concurred uninterestedly, without making any attempt to either get up, or look up.

'Are you hungry?' he quizzed, squatting on his haunches beside her.

Alix completed her latest drawing before shaking her head. 'Not very. Are you?'

'A little.'

Still without having looked at him she tossed the driftwood back into the sea and rose to her feet, brushing the sand away from her legs and the seat of her costume in quick nervous movements.

'We may as well have something,' she proposed quietly. 'It's probably time for lunch anyway.'

She was only allowed to take a couple of steps before a hard hand slid beneath her wet hair to grasp the nape of her neck and forcibly turn her face upwards.

'Are you deliberately trying to rile me, Alix?' he lowered his head to demand softly.

'No, of course not,' she denied almost tearfully. 'What would I have to gain from doing that?'

'That's what I keep asking myself,' he countered heavily.

There didn't seem to be any return she could give to that and she stood uncomfortably beneath his analytical gaze until, at last, he let go of her and she was able to continue on her way towards the row of sheltering palms. Hastily, she took deep fried chicken legs, prepared salad vegetables, and fresh bread rolls from the cold chest and arranged them appetisingly on plates set out on the cloth-covered tartan rug.

'Food's ready,' she called to where Kirby still stood

at the water's edge looking down at the last picture she had drawn in the sand.

He raised one hand in acknowledgement and walked back up the beach with a lithe stride which involuntarily fascinated her with its vital self-assurance.

'As I remember, you had quite a flair for drawing,' he remarked thoughtfully, lowering himself down on the opposite side of the rug to her. 'Did you ever get around to taking that arts course you used to talk about?'

'No, there didn't seem to be the time,' she shrugged.

'Too many men friends?'

Alix shot him an anguished look. He seemed to say it so casually! As if he really couldn't have cared less how many men she had dated during the years of their separation.

'No,' she answered flatly. 'Too many hours working.'

Kirby bit appreciatively into a drumstick and chewed for a few moments. 'In the same supermarket where you worked before we met?'

'That's right.' She was surprised he remembered.

'Doing what?'

'Pricing in the stock room originally, then as a check-out operator, and now as assistant to the manager,' she relayed tonelessly.

His head dipped in a wry kind of salute. 'Sounds impressive.'

'More impressive than my wages are,' she owned ruefully. 'Or perhaps I should have said "were". I don't know how much leave of absence they'll give me before getting in a permanent replacement. They've been very good so far, but I can't expect them to hold the position open for me indefinitely.'

Kirby's eyes ranged intently over her pensive face. 'You don't sound as if you care much,' he charged.

Alix hunched her shoulders indifferently. 'If I said I did, you still wouldn't fly me home, so what's the use? Anyway, if it comes to the worst there are other supermarkets, closer to home, where it might be more convenient to work.'

'You think you'll be able to find a similar job that easily?'

'How should I know?' she flashed irritably. She had enough trouble dealing with present problems without imagining those she might encounter in the future. 'I'll have to wait and see what happens with this position first, won't I?'

'Okay, okay, I'm sorry I asked,' he held up one hand in an arresting motion, his tone decidedly colder. 'I was trying to take an interest, that's all.'

The opportunity was too good to pass up and Alix pounced on it, gibing, 'Then you're four years too late, Kirby! The time for you to have shown an interest was when we were first married ... not now we're getting a divorce!'

By the menacing expression on his savagely set face Alix was positive he would have murdered her if he had thought he could have got away with it, and she even moved backwards on the rug in anticipation of a physical retaliation which didn't eventuate. His words when they came were hardly less destructive, however.

'And maybe—just maybe—it's only now that we're divorcing that I consider you're worth any interest!' he lashed back at her derisively.

With a choking sob and her eyes filling with blinding tears, Alix whirled to her feet and ran, heading instinctively for the shelter of the rocks at the head of the sandspit and stumbling around the first barrier before collapsing against a smoothly eroded boulder and weeping bitterly, unmindful of the seabirds wheeling overhead or the incoming tide.

It was only much later, when the sea crept around her ankles with an insidious gurgle, that she realised her position would soon be untenable, and after splashing handfuls of water over her flushed face and combing her fingers through her hair to straighten some of the tangles she reluctantly returned to the open beach.

As she neared the trees she could see that their picnic things had been replaced in the chest and Kirby was lying face down on the rug, his head resting comfortably on his folded arms, his eyes closed. A few yards away she halted and surveyed the lean hard body, noting the powerfully moulded arms and back, the slim waist, the strongly muscled legs, and feeling once again that aching surge of longing for what might have been. Perhaps she sighed aloud, but suddenly his eyes flicked open and she was transfixed by a piercing blue stare.

'I'm sorry if I disturbed you,' she murmured stiffly, licking at her salty lips. 'Is there any drink left?'

He rolled on to his side, supporting his weight on one elbow. 'Help yourself,' he proposed sardonically.

Nervously, Alix did as he suggested, but still managed to savour the clean tang of the cold fruit juice as it trickled down her taut throat. In returning the flask and her mug she bent to fasten the clips on the chest and a hand whipped out to catch at her forearm and topple her on to the rug.

In the frantic struggle which ensued Kirby effortlessly emerged the victor by the simple expedient of kneeling astride her thrashing body and pinning her wrists to the ground on either side of her head.

Exhausted, and with her breath coming in deep shuddering gasps which made her breasts rise and fall rapidly beneath their flimsy covering, Alix could only fasten her eyes to his imploringly. She had no idea what his intentions were, but in his present mood she guessed anything was possible.

For his part, Kirby's own breathing was none too steady as he stared down into the aquamarine eyes pleading so eloquently with him and he gritted his teeth together wrathfully.

'Just what the hell *do* you want of me, then, Alix?' he smouldered. '*This* . . .?'

As his head lowered Alix immediately resumed her fight in a panicking kind of desperation, but he overcame her renewed resistance as easily as he had her previous opposition and his mouth claimed hers roughly, ravaging it with long devouring kisses which hurt and yet excited at the same time.

His ability to arouse her sexually had always been a most satisfying part of their marriage, but it frightened Alix now and dry sobs of despair began gathering at the back of her throat. She knew her lips to be softening beneath the ruthless pressure and she twisted jerkily in a last distraught effort to break free. He was deliberately using his undoubted mastery to ignite a consuming flame of desire within her and he was succeeding. She ached from head to toe with an unfulfilled yearning and she felt dizzy with the strength of her own ungovernable emotions.

'Oh, please ...!' she groaned helplessly when Kirby's lips wandered unchecked across her burning cheeks to seek the vulnerable lobe of her ear and the tip of his tongue tormented the throbbing cord at the side of her neck.

His response to her plea was to sensually take possession of her parted lips again and to gradually lower his hard form along her quivering length, finally freeing one of her wrists in order to run his hand exploringly over her soft flesh. Alix knew she should have used the opportunity to strike out at him—to make another, stronger, bid to tear loose—but she was deaf to her mind's urgings and she arched against him pliantly, her fingers clasping at wide shoulders as she surrendered to the pleasures of his persuasive touch.

Only when she felt the halter strap of her bikini untied and the material being pushed aside did her head begin to assert its authority and she clutched a covering hand to her exposed breast with a vehement, '*No!*' of protest on her lips.

Kirby's eyes, only inches from her own, glittered icily and for a moment Alix quakingly believed he meant to ignore her objection and force her compliance—which she was all too aware he could have done had he so chosen, for she certainly didn't have the strength to stop him—but then, with a almost contemptuous lift to one corner of his mouth, he flexed one shoulder indifferently and rolled agilely to his feet.

This time it was Alix who was left sitting on the rug, following his path to the sea with a pained gaze and watching as he struck out strongly through the first line of breakers. Swiftly she retied her halter and then stared moodily at the sand she was digging her fingers into.

Perhaps even greater than her humiliation in knowing she had yielded so readily to his seductive caresses was the recollection of his disparaging leavetaking. That caused the deepest ache of all, she discovered. And why? She shifted uncomfortably, not wanting to analyse her feelings any further, but her thoughts wouldn't be denied now that they were finally in control and she couldn't refuse to listen to the logical reasoning of her brain any longer. Because she was still in love with him, that was why!

She might have liked to tell herself she wasn't, pretend she didn't mind if he divorced her, facetiously offer him to Melanie, but no matter what she said or did to the contrary the facts were irrefutable. She did care. Oh, God, how she cared! She was as much in love with him now as she had ever been and that was the reason for the agonising hurt his scornful departure had created. What hope did she have when her husband obviously thought so little of her? His love hadn't endured during four lonely years that was for certain. His hadn't been lonely ones, she recalled desolately.

Their journey home, not unexpectedly, was completed without a word being spoken. When Kirby had returned from his swim Alix was already dressed and waiting by the car, an indication of her wish to leave as soon as possible against which he didn't demur. He had merely rubbed himself roughly dry with a towel and pulled on a pair of slim-fitting shorts over his wet costume and slid into the driving seat, apparently considering even the time it would have taken to drag on his shirt to be wasteful in his desire to be rid of her company.

On their arrival at Maiyatta Alix retreated to the kitchen to unpack, still without having opened her mouth, and that seemed to set the pattern for the days to come. They spoke to each other if it was absolutely imperative, but definitely not otherwise.

CHAPTER SIX

FOR Alix, the following month brought great changes, at least outwardly. Her figure began to noticeably regain its natural curving contours and her physical health improved tremendously, although the same couldn't have been said for her emotional state. It remained depressingly low. In fact, apart from when she had been most ill in the hospital Alix couldn't remember a time when she had felt quite so despondent, and this made it all the more difficult to appear unconcerned by Kirby's silences and Melanie's taunting inferences.

In her endeavours to avoid both of them she had taken to leaving the property as often as she could. She had visited waterfalls and lookouts; tramped through rain forests and along beaches until she had been to every scenic area in the district; driven in to town on numerous occasions for no particular reason so that her face was becoming quite familiar to many of the residents; and even been persuaded by Karen Aylward—who had proved to be a good friend—to accompany her to some local women's meetings.

To her surprise she had found these thoroughly enjoyable and not at all composed of 'a lot of stuffy old women discussing recipes and their children's latest illnesses' as she had once, ignorantly, denounced to Kirby. Their discussions had been varied and ably presented, and she found herself willingly taking an interest in such things as weaving, pottery, macramé, and of course the inevitable fund raising for the many charities they supported.

It was after one of their meetings that Karen prompted, 'You won't forget the party tonight, will you?' as they headed for their respective cars.

'No, of course I won't,' Alix assured her. The party was being given to celebrate Karen's brother Simon's engagement. 'Although I can't guarantee that Kirby will be very pleasant company. Or, at least, not while he's with me,' she amended ruefully.

'Well, if he doesn't treat you nicely while you're in our house I'll get Tim to say a few words to him,' Karen threatened loyally.

Apart from seeing him a couple of times on the road and passing a few commonplace remarks when he had come home one afternoon just as she was leaving the Aylward property, Alix hadn't spoken to Tim since the day they met, but she still didn't think it advisable for her friend to carry out her promise.

'Good grief, don't do that,' she exhorted wryly. 'I wouldn't like to be the cause of breaking their friendship. Besides, it's not that Kirby doesn't treat me nicely, he just doesn't speak, that's all.'

'Well, what would you call that, if it's not unpleasant?'

'A respite,' Alix laughed hollowly, grimacing. 'Believe me, it's less pleasant when we're talking to one another.'

'Oh, Alix, you sound so uncaring,' her friend mourned with a sigh. 'Wouldn't you really like a reconciliation?'

'No,' she lied. There weren't many things she had kept secret from Karen, but the truth of her real feelings regarding her husband was one of them. 'In any case, aren't you forgetting Melanie? Kirby's already made his choice as to which of us he would prefer as his wife,' with a smile which belied the unbearable hurt it caused her to make the remark.

'But he preferred you first!'

'Four years ago, maybe. Since then, however, I rather think I've disappointed him somewhat,' she confessed drily, the sting of self-mockery in her words.

'You were only eighteen,' Karen tried to make excuses for her. 'He could hardly have expected perfection.'

'No, but he was entitled to expect a better wife than he got,' Alix admitted honestly. She had done some hard thinking on that point in the last few weeks. Then, as she reached her car, 'I'm sorry if I'm destroying your theory on true love overcoming all difficulties,' she smiled ruefully. 'Let's hope Simon has better luck with his choice.'

'Oh, yes, the party.' Karen was easily distracted. 'We'll see you about eightish, right?'

'Stop worrying, we'll be there. We may not be talking, but we *will* be there,' she confirmed sardonically.

As Alix dressed for the occasion after a discomfiting dinner spent with an unsociable Kirby she was grateful she could find something to be pleased about. Now that she had regained her lost weight her best evening dress fitted her like a dream. It was of a one-shouldered design which fitted snugly to her slender waist and then fell in becoming folds to the floor. The skirt and back were of black chiffon, but the front of the bodice consisted of a series of two inch stripes running diagonally from shoulder to waist in a rainbow variety of bright colours.

Her hair she drew back severely from her high forehead and then pinned it into a coronet of curls, and her make-up was applied with the hand of an artist. There was no need for a foundation now that her skin was lightly tanned and the hollows had disappeared, but she did darken her brows and eyelashes and add a touch of frost green shadow to her lids to emphasise the colour of her eyes. Her mouth she coated with a clear glossy coral. Next she clipped a pair of long gold drop earrings into place and then liberally sprayed herself with icy cologne.

Stepping back from the mirror she eyed the satisfying result drily. The pity of it was ... it was all for nothing, she sighed, and scooped up a gold drawstring evening purse from the dressing table before heading for the door.

Kirby was finishing a drink in the sitting room when she walked in, a half smoked cigarette between his fingers. In evening clothes he was devastating and momentarily Alix closed her eyes to hide the despair she felt sure was written there.

'For Tim?'

The sarcastic drawl had her opening them again swiftly and discovering him to be making a pointed assessment of her appearance. Angrily, she allowed her glance to appraise him just as satirically.

'For Melly?' she countered, eyes widening pertly.

'And if it is?'

Alix looked uninterested although she had no idea how she managed it. 'Then I'm sure she'll be very proud. You look . . .' her voice almost failed her, but she held it together long enough to murmured, 'very classy.'

He acknowledged her compliment with an indolent tilt of his head. 'And you, my love, are going to be the most stunningly beautiful female there tonight,' he advised in turn, his compelling eyes never leaving her surprised ones as he slowly walked towards her. When he reached her side he stubbed out his cigarette in an ashtray and then tilted her face firmly up to his to caution, 'Just don't make the mistake of forgetting whose brand you carry, hmm?'

'I'm not one of your stud cattle, Kirby, I don't happen to carry a brand!' she retorted with a rebellious glare.

'No?' His expression hardened fractionally. 'Then you'd better think again, because those are *my* rings you're wearing.'

'But only on my fingers . . . not through my nose!'

For the first time since Alix had returned to Maiyatta she saw Kirby really laugh and the effect it had
on her was so shattering that she couldn't drag her
wistful eyes away. That was, not until Kirby had
sobered enough to bait, 'You keep looking at me like
that, my love, and we won't even make it to the
party.'

Alix couldn't have whirled out of his reach faster if
someone had told her there was a deadly snake behind her. 'I'm sorry, I can assure you it wasn't inten-
tional,' she declared stiltedly, apprehensively.

'So I gathered,' he drawled ironically, and finished
his drink.

'Yes, well ...' She moved restlessly from one foot
to the other. She preferred his silences to this type of
taunting conversation. He was far too unpredictable
for her to dare answer in kind. 'Shall we go?' she
queried hopefully, gathering up a brightly papered
parcel from the table.

'After you,' he smiled wryly, and Alix took him up
on his offer without hesitation.

The drive to the Aylwards' property was quickly
accomplished, and minus any more of Kirby's provoking comments, for which Alix was very grateful.
The house—built as a haven from the heat with wide
verandahs, big windows, and even bigger doors—appeared filled with people as they parked the car, and
the gaily chattering throng had already begun to spill
out into the colourfully lit gardens. Alix knew from
what Karen had told her that most of the district had

been invited, but even so she hadn't expected there to be such a crowd and she unconsciously moved closer to Kirby's side. She had always found it a little uncomfortable to attend a gathering where she knew very few of those present.

As it turned out, however, she needn't have worried because she soon discovered she knew far more people than she had realised. She had forgotten the friendly faces—a lot of them she still couldn't put a name to—she had come to know through club meetings and between their and Kirby's introductions it was only a matter of time before her circle of acquaintances had grown considerably larger.

Inside the house some areas were cleared for dancing while others had been set aside for those who just wished to sit and talk, and it was to one of these that Kirby guided her after they had been greeted by their host and hostess and Alix had been introduced to Simon and his fiancée, Veronica, to whom she had handed their gift-wrapped package, along with her sincere best wishes.

They had only been seated for a few moments and Alix was approving of the fruit punch Kirby had procured for her when she saw Melanie arrive with her parents, detach herself immediately, and head unerringly in their direction. In multi-checked Thai silk, Alix had to concede, though grudgingly, that Melanie did indeed look extremely stylish.

'Hello, there!' she greeted them both gaily, although her eyes were raking over Alix minutely. 'My,

I must say you look very attractive tonight, Alix. What do you reckon, boss?' as she calmly perched herself on the arm of his chair.

'I've already told Alix what I think,' Kirby answered her drily, while his wife did her best to keep her dislike from showing. Melanie was always sweet and gushing when Kirby was around.

But not to be outdone, she forced a smile on to her lips to enthuse, 'Your dress is very becoming too, Melly. Those colours suit you very well.'

'Mmm, they do, don't they?' The other girl wasn't above capitalising on the comment by doing a model turn in order to demonstrate the wide expanse of bare skin the plunging back exposed, but as music floated out from the next room she bent to the man beside her engagingly. 'Come and trip the light fantastic with me, boss. I probably won't get another chance all evening.' Her eyes slid goadingly across to Alix and she continued, 'You'll be too busy warding off your wife's many admirers.'

When Kirby hesitated, Alix made the decision for him. 'That's all right, you go ahead,' she recommended with false brightness, immediately springing to her feet and looking over the crowded dance floor. 'I wanted to see Karen about something anyway. I'll see you later.'

Before giving either of them a chance to speak Alix had spun on her heel and walked out, and she was still looking for the green dress Karen had said she would be wearing when a barring arm halted her progress and a disappointed voice asked, 'Aren't you even going to talk to me?'

On recognising the owner of the arm Alix laughed. 'I'm sorry, Tim, I really didn't see you. I was looking for your sister.'

'Apology accepted,' he grinned, and drew her towards the two young men he had been conversing with. 'You haven't met my other brothers yet, have you? David and Peter—Alix Whitman,' he indicated in turn.

'I'm pleased to meet you at last,' she smiled genuinely at each of them. 'Karen's told me a lot about you.'

'Sounds ominous,' David exchanged grins with his brothers.

By the time Alix had laughingly disabused them of their preconceived notions another dance was in progress and Tim invited her on to the floor.

'Look, I'm sorry about that trip I promised you to the mill,' he said as they moved slowly among the other dancers. 'Did Kirby actually get around to taking you?'

'Yes, it was very interesting,' she nodded, not wanting to remember what had happened afterwards. 'But you don't have to apologise, it wasn't your fault. I had no idea Kirby would suddenly feel the need to assert himself like that.'

'I thought it more than likely,' Tim chuckled.

'You did?'

'Uh-huh! I was just surprised it took him till that

morning before telling me to keep my hands off his property.'

His *property*! How dared he! Alix seethed. But to her partner her words were a little less fiery.

'Well, he had no right to say anything of the sort, you were only being obliging.' Her soft lips twisted ruefully. 'I guess it's my turn to apologise now for getting you mixed up in our private quarrels.'

'There's no need,' he reassured her with a grin. 'You just misjudged the strength of your husband's proprietorial instincts, that's all.'

What he really meant was his damned *pride*, Alix corrected acidly. Kirby had no proprietorial instincts where she was concerned, only an aversion to anyone knowing she preferred someone else's company.

Apparently it *was* acceptable for him to flaunt his interest in Melanie in public, though. This was the second dance in a row they'd had together now, she noted, her eyes clouding mistily as her vision locked on her husband and his secretary some distance away, Kirby's expression attentive as he listened to what his sparkling partner was saying. Suddenly, as his head lifted unexpectedly, Alix found a glacial blue stare returning her somewhat reproachful survey and, averting her eyes quickly, she gave Tim a contrite smile.

'Would you mind very much if we adjourned to the verandah for a drink?' she requested faintly.

'Of course not.' His eyes roved anxiously over her taut features. 'Aren't you feeling too good?'

'It—it's the heat,' she prevaricated, although it

wasn't an overly warm night. 'You probably don't notice it, but I'm sorry, I'm not quite used to it yet.'

Tim put his arm around her in concern and began escorting her from the room. 'That's okay,' he smiled encouragingly. 'The rain we had earlier in the week probably hasn't helped any. A lot of people find it difficult to acclimatise to our high humidity.'

Shamefaced for deceiving him when all she had wanted to do was to escape from her husband's distressing presence, Alix only nodded and gratefully accepted the chair he held out for her. At least while she was outside she was spared the humiliating experience of seeing Kirby holding Melanie in his arms.

It wasn't long before Tim was back with a drink for her, bringing Karen and her latest boy-friend, Cliff, with him, and in a very short while the four of them had been joined by a number of lively friends all willing to ensure there wasn't a lull in the conversation or the laughter. It was after someone had recounted a particularly funny story which had produced a prolonged roar of amusement that Alix became aware of a figure beside her chair and with a wide smile still on her lips she looked up to see who it might be.

'Good on you, Kirby, have you come to join us?' a male voice called out as Alix's smile began to fade slightly.

'No, thanks, Ned,' he shook his head. 'I've come to claim my wife for a dance ... if she'll allow me to drag her away from all of you, that is.'

Alix laughed along with the rest of them—there wasn't much else she could do without creating a scene—but as she rose to her feet and turned towards him it was to gibe tartly from the corner of her mouth, 'Is poor dear Melly exhausted already, then?' before facing the others again and promising, 'I'll be back, so keep a seat vacant.'

Kirby's fingers bit deeply into her upper arm as they walked through to the lounge. 'And just what did you mean by that crack?' he demanded softly.

'I should have thought it was painfully obvious.' She cast him a highly sardonic glance from beneath her thick lashes. 'You wouldn't be asking me to dance if darling Melly was still available, would you?'

'Wouldn't I? You didn't stay around long enough to find out!' he grated, anger emanating from him like an invisible vapour. 'The minute we arrived you set off supposedly to look for Karen, but which was just an excuse to find Tim! Then, immediately I see you with him, you can't get out of the room fast enough in order to set up your own little court on the verandah!'

'Oh, that's ridiculous!' she retorted scornfully. 'I was one of a group, nothing more.'

'Of which you just happened to be the only one who's married!'

'So can I help it if my husband prefers dancing with his secretary?' she goaded dulcetly.

Kirby jerked her sharply into his arms and they automatically began to move to the music. 'You can when you use it as an excuse to pretend to go looking for Karen!' he accused.

'It wasn't an excuse. I did look for her.'

'But conveniently found Tim instead!' His brows peaked expressively.

'Not conveniently ... accidentally,' she countered smartly.

He uttered a short disparaging sound. 'Do you honestly expect me to believe that?'

'Actually, I don't give a damn whether you do or not,' she flashed stormily. 'But if you're planning on gazing soulfully into Melly's big brown eyes all evening, then don't expect me to be hanging around to watch the sickening display, because I just won't be there!'

'Oh, and where *will* you be?' he enquired silkily, forebodingly.

Alix deliberately tipped her face up to his, a slow secretive smile giving her perfectly formed countenance an air of provocation. 'Guess?' she invited mockingly.

Retaliation was immediate. Kirby stopped dancing and pulled her hard against him, one hand swiftly spanning her chin and immobilising it in its tilted position.

'Are you challenging me, my love?' he bent his head to whisper close to her parted lips.

A deep flush mounted her cheeks as she imagined the sight they presented and had her ordering frantically, 'Stop it, Kirby! Everyone's looking at us.'

'Mmm, but they'll just think I'm so captivated by my beautiful wife that I can't help myself,' he drawled with an aggravating smile as his thumb began to caress the soft underside of her jaw.

The discreet efforts to struggle free that Alix could make were totally ineffective and she glared furiously into the depths of his gleaming blue eyes. 'They'll know differently if you force me to slap that mocking face of yours!' she vowed heatedly.

'And if you do I shall have no compunction in turning you over my knee right here and now in the middle of the dance floor,' he smiled so lovingly at her that none of the other guests could possibly tell it was a threat he was issuing.

He was capable of it, Alix fumed, but whether he would or not she couldn't be sure and, consequently, she had no recourse but to resort to pleading.

'Kirby, please! Couldn't we settle our difference somewhere a little less public?' she begged.

At last, after what seemed to be an eternity to Alix, a sardonic look pulled at his mouth as he freed her and they began moving again, much to her sighed relief.

'Isn't it a little late for you to be worrying about appearances when you've had everyone thinking you were Tim's newest girl-friend up until now?' he jeered.

Alix's eyes widened in disbelief. 'Oh, but they couldn't have,' she gasped. 'I—I've done nothing to make them think that.'

'Except sit next to him all evening.'

'That's not fair,' she cried resentfully. 'What was I supposed to do, sit on my own?'

The hand at her waist dug a little deeper. 'How about with your husband, or didn't that occur to you?'

'You were dancing with Melly!' indignantly.

'I wonder why?' There was a hint of anger amidst the irony.

Alix stared at him in confusion. She would have thought an answer to that question was unnecessary. 'Well, because she asked you, I suppose,' she offered, perplexed.

'And if I hadn't planned to accept?'

If she had been confused before, now she was confounded as well. Not accept? It was unthinkable! And further than that her floundering thoughts couldn't go.

'Oh, don't assume such a dumbfounded expression, Alix,' he censured disgustedly. 'You knew damned well I had no intention of leaving you on your own so soon after arriving. Why not be honest enough to admit you just wanted to seek Tim out?'

'Because I didn't!' she hissed. 'And how would I have a clue as to what you intended? You've always seemed anxious enough to be with her before. Don't tell me she's beginning to pall ... *already*!'

Ebony lashes lowered to give his face a distinctly contemptuous cast. 'No, there's only one female I've had a gutful of ... and that's my malicious, hypocritical *wife*!'

'Then why don't you do yourself a favour and go back to your ever-loving secretary?' she recommended sarcastically, refusing to permit even the smallest part of her hurt to show. 'I'm sure she'll welcome you with open arms.'

'The same way you're hoping Tim will welcome you?' he lashed at her savagely.

His incensed reaction was like balm to her wounded spirit and, purposely seeking to goad him further, Alix raised one shoulder with unavoidable meaning in response to his rancorous probing and then, when his eyes threatened an unbridled eruption, purred mockingly, 'You're forgetting to smile, darling. People won't think you're captivated by your beautiful wife any more if you don't keep smiling.'

'Then I shall have to do something else to convince them, shan't I?' he ground out through clenched teeth and, whirling her out on to the verandah, set his mouth to hers in a roughly abrasive kiss.

To have fought him would only have brought greater humiliation and embarrassment and so, despite her fury, Alix was forced to suffer his unsparing possession of her lips until it suited Kirby to release her. And that wasn't for some considerable time.

'There, I think that should have made it perfectly clear just who you belong to,' he taunted as his arms finally slid away from her.

'You—you ...!'

always knows exactly what he's doing.'

Which was more than Alix did at the moment because Karen's remark had just left her wondering. She didn't want Tim getting any ideas of an amorous persuasion just because she and Kirby were separated, but as there had been nothing in his attitude so far to suggest that he might be, she eventually decided to accept the invitation.

'Then thank you, I'd like that very much,' she smiled.

For the rest of the afternoon their talk centred around the pioneer cottage which the local Historical Society—of which both Karen and Tim were members—was buying with the intention of restoring it to its original condition, filling it with the various artefacts the Society had collected over the years, and then opening it to the public as a museum. Apparently the purchase was almost completed and the members were extremely eager to help with the renovations.

Karen suggested that Alix might like to go along to help too and, to her surprise, Alix found herself agreeing without hesitation. At least it was another way in which to escape from the repressive atmosphere of Maiyatta, she mused wryly.

Their second swim, much later in the afternoon, was as pleasant as their first and as the time was being passed in such congenial company none of them showed any desire to leave until the sun was very low behind them, and even then Alix was reluctant to move. The day had been thoroughly enjoyable and she didn't want it to end—especially not by spending the last few remaining hours with an uncommunicative husband!

Nevertheless, she was perfectly aware it would have to end some time and with a sigh she walked back to the car and slipped her dress on over the top of her bikini. It was well and truly dry, so there wasn't much point in fumbling around in the car, changing, when there was no pressing need. As Karen and Tim lived some five miles further along the Roslyndale road they followed Alix all the way to her turn-off, then with the acknowledging sound of Tim's horn in response to her wave, she continued on to the house.

After garaging the car and stacking her parcels in one arm it was only due to the blaze of light spilling out through the windows and doorway that Alix was able to pick her way safely through the garden, for it was completely dark now, with no moon at all as yet to relieve the blackness. But as she mounted the steps Kirby's tall figure rose immediately from one of the wicker chairs placed around the verandah and came to stand beside the front doorway with his hands on his hips, his thunderous expression dark enough to rival the coal black sky.

'And might I ask, just where the hell you've been?' he rasped in a low tone.

'I told you where I was going this morning.' Alix's brows arched in astonishment. 'I went to Roslyndale.'

'Until this hour? You said you would be back early in the afternoon!'

There were so many names Alix would have liked to call him that she couldn't decide which was the most appropriate one to use first, but before she could voice any of them Kirby was smiling and drawling,

'Tut-tut, my love, now you've forgotten *your* smile ... and everyone's watching you.'

The timely reminder brought her up short and she managed to relax her stormy expression, if not her clenching fingers. 'You know something!' she mouthed direfully, but accompanied it with a camouflaging smile. 'Male chauvinist pig is much too courteous a description for you!'

Kirby's laughter was still ringing annoyingly in her ears when Alix resumed her seat at the table, and the joking remark, 'I wish someone would thank *me* for a dance like that!' from a redhead three seats along, didn't help to dispel her anger at his treatment. When the incident had died a natural death and the talk had returned to other topics Tim leant across the arm of his chair, ostensibly to refill her glass from the jug of punch.

'Those instincts at work again?' he quizzed drily.

'Something like that,' she grimaced, without admitting to him, or herself, that her goading might have had a hand in initiating it. 'He's becoming more impossible as the days pass. We either don't speak at all, or we fight like cat and dog, there's never anything in between. I don't know why he doesn't file his divorce and get it over and done with.'

'Why don't you, if you feel so strongly about it?'

'I probably would if I wasn't, to all intents and purposes, a guest in his house,' she lied brazenly. Even after this last incident, feeling as she did about him she could never willingly instigate a procedure which would irrevocably part them. 'It would be rather like biting the hand that's feeding you, don't you think?'

'Perhaps,' he shrugged wryly. 'And then again, perhaps neither of you is as anxious to make the break as you think you are. I mean, you've already had four years in which to do something about it, and yet you're still as legally tied as ever you were.'

'But only by coincidence, certainly not design,' she insisted promptly. 'There didn't seem any pressing need on my part since I hadn't expected to see him again—apart from the fact that until this year I really couldn't afford to do anything about it—and Kirby ... well, I rather think he found it convenient until now.'

'Why now, in particular?' he frowned.

Alix hunched one shoulder and fiddled with her purse on the table. Why should she try and keep it a secret, soon everyone would know. 'Because he has now come to a decision regarding my replacement.'

'Your replacement?' The furrows across Tim's forehead grew even deeper. 'You're having me on!'

'No, I have it straight from the horse's mouth,' she grimaced, a superhuman effort needed to keep her tone casual.

'*Kirby* told you?' he stared at her incredulously.

'Not in so many words, but his girl-friend wasn't so backward.'

He looked more nonplussed now than he had previously. 'And might I ask just who that is?' he probed.

Turning in her seat, Alix indicated the girl who was catching so possessively at Kirby's arm while he talked to Simon and Veronica.

'His one and only faultless and indispensable helping hand, Melanie Gordon, naturally,' she gibed.

To have said Tim appeared taken aback would have been an understatement. Clearly, he was staggered.

'Well, that would have to be the best kept secret of all time,' he snorted, not without a tinge of scepticism. 'I haven't heard even a whisper about it and I'll warrant no one else has either.' Halting, he peered at her intently. 'Are you positive you've got your facts right?'

Alix shrugged uninterestedly. 'I only know what I'm told, and Melanie certainly didn't seem to have any doubts on the matter.'

Tim rocked his chair on to its back legs, his fingers linking behind his head, his eyes slanting sideways with a considering look. 'But Kirby's said nothing definite?' he queried.

'He doesn't have to,' Alix laughed bleakly. 'I can read between the lines easily enough. It's all there in black and white if you know where to look.'

Tim let out his breath slowly and allowed his chair

to sink level again but before he could sound her with any more of his unwittingly hurtful questions Karen had stood up and was remarking, 'As it will be time for supper soon I'd better see about giving Mum a hand.'

'I'll help you,' Alix offered swiftly, glad of the chance to occupy her mind with more mundane thoughts and moving to join the other girl as the ensuing exclamations of, 'So will I,' and, 'Me too,' indicated it would be a case of many hands making light work.

Except for a few laughing quips and comments as they passed each other on their way back and forth from the kitchen to the side verandah where tables had been made ready to receive the appetising food, there wasn't much opportunity for talking and not until the last dish, overflowing with shelled King prawns, was heading towards its final resting place did Karen manage to single Alix out.

'I know you said you and Kirby probably wouldn't be talking, but except for that one dance he ended with a sizzling kiss—which, I gather, you didn't exactly approve of—he hasn't been near you all evening. I thought he would at least have pretended to keep you company,' she whispered accusingly as they also made their way slowly to the verandah.

Poor Karen, Alix sighed ruefully, she really was loath to accept her and Kirby's present incompatibility. Besides, the distance they had been keeping from one another this evening had been as much her doing as his, if not more.

'There wouldn't be much point considering the way we snap and snarl at each other,' she reasoned plausibly. 'I wouldn't like to subject all and sundry to our continual arguments.'

'You'd think he could have made an exception for one night, though. Surely that wouldn't have been asking too much?'

About to make a gibing reply, Alix abruptly refrained as the subject of their conversation suddenly materialised beside them via the french doors leading to the lounge.

'You sound very indignant, young Karen,' Kirby smiled lazily. 'Who's been rubbing you the wrong way tonight?'

'You have, Kirby Whitman,' was the immediate retort which had Alix staring aghast at her friend and making frantic vetoing motions with one hand, but which were pointedly ignored as Karen continued righteously, 'I think it's dreadful you couldn't make the effort to be nice to your wife for one evening instead of leaving her on her own all the time.'

A measuring look came to rest on Alix's apprehensive face and then swung back to Karen again, a wry curve shaping firmly moulded lips. 'On her own?' he repeated sardonically.

'Oh, you know what I mean,' the younger girl returned, undaunted. 'You should have been the one sitting next to her, not Tim.'

'Karen!' Alix broke in faintly, horrified at the turn

the conversation was taking, but only to find her remonstrance being ignored as Kirby advised mockingly,

'But Alix prefers it that way. Didn't she tell you?'

'I'm not surprised if you keep picking quarrels with her,' Karen countered doggedly. 'But I'm sure it would be an entirely different story if you put yourself out to be pleasant for a change.'

'Oh?' One dark eyebrow arched meaningfully as assessing eyes were once again turned in his wife's direction.

Alix's gaze darted to each of them in turn, first reproachfully, and then embarrassedly. 'I'm s-sorry, Karen had no right to imply any such thing,' she murmured huskily, her cheeks reddening.

'You mean, you would rather I wasn't pleasant?'

'Of course not,' she denied mechanically, then chewed at her lip, flustered. She had the strangest feeling of being manipulated. 'I only meant ...'

'Then how can I refuse?' Kirby interrupted in a drawl. It sounded sarcastic to Alix's ears. 'I shall be my wife's constant companion for the remainder of the evening.' He flicked an enquiring glance at Karen and grinned, 'That better?'

'Much,' she laughed, a satisfied expression on her face.

'Oh, look, there's really no need for all this,' it was left to Alix to protest diffidently. 'I'm not asking for any pity.'

Kirby linked her arm with his and began escorting

them both towards the laden tables where a crowd had started gathering.

'You're not getting any,' he advised drily. 'I am merely fulfilling my duty as your husband at Karen's request.'

'Then I—I waive that duty on your behalf.' She was beginning to panic and she knew it, but the thought of him going out of his way to be nice to her was already creating an inward turmoil she couldn't control. 'I'm quite capable of taking care of myself, thank you.'

'Mmm, but as Karen rightly pointed out, you shouldn't have to while I'm here, should you?' he baited, eyes dancing with a gleaming light she knew so well.

With a vexed sigh for her friend's well-intentioned but unwanted interference, Alix acknowledged defeat despairingly. It was obvious Kirby was determined to play the part of the attentive husband and, apart from drawing humiliating attention to them, there appeared to be very little she could do about it. Why he had chosen to accept Karen's rebuke so readily and in such good humour she had no idea, although she suspected sheer perverseness had been a strong contributing factor, but if she was to survive the situation with any remnants of her pride and self-respect undamaged then she was going to have to guard her feelings closely. She was only too aware of the catastrophic effect Kirby could have on her volatile emotions if he deliberately set out to be charming.

'There, isn't that nicer?' questioned Karen, pleasure evident in her tone, as they waited on a cane sofa for Kirby and Cliff to return from the buffet tables.

'Not really,' Alix half laughed wryly.

'Oh, but I thought ...' Pausing, Karen frowned. 'Even if you don't want a reconciliation, surely you would prefer an amicable divorce?'

Amicable! Alix grimaced. What a feeble term to describe the aftermath of the devouring spark and fire which drew two people into a passionate union such as theirs had been. Or ... or had Karen unwittingly put her finger on the reason for Kirby's sudden about-face in attitude? Had his change really been brought about by perverseness ... or artfulness? He wanted an uncontested divorce, and what better way to achieve it than by being on amiable terms with his wife!

The thought buzzed around in her brain like an angry bee at discovering itself encaged. So that was the game he meant to play, was it? she seethed, her breasts heaving. Well, he would find she wasn't so accommodating as to be taken in by such an underhanded little ploy. In fact, he could very well find she was capable of being as contrary and difficult as he was!

In reply to Karen's query she moved one lightly tanned shoulder in an indifferent gesture and agreed, 'I guess so.'

'You guess so!' Karen's eyes opened wide and then she blinked in surprise. 'Good grief, you amaze me sometimes, Alix! What sort of an answer is that? Don't you *want* to be on friendly terms with Kirby?'

'Now that you've asked ... no, I don't!' came the swift denial. 'And nor do I want a friendly divorce or a friendly settlement. And why not? Because I intend to fight him every step of the way!'

'Alix, you can't mean that!' Karen cried, shocked. 'It—it doesn't make sense. You've never mentioned anything about this before. Why the sudden change of heart now?'

'There's been no change, only a hardening of my resolve,' Alix told her levelly. 'Kirby knows I don't mean to make things easy for him and Melanie. Why else do you think he agreed so willingly to keep me company this evening? Because he's hoping thereby to persuade me to do otherwise, of course!'

'I don't believe it! Kirby's just not capable of doing something so treacherous,' Karen declared staunchly.

'All's fair in love and war, they say,' Alix shrugged impassively.

'Well, I still don't believe it. You've got it wrong somehow. You must have.'

Alix wished she had, but unfortunately her inner conviction was just too strong to be gainsaid. What other reason could there possibly be for his demeanour to have altered so startlingly? There wasn't one that she could fathom.

CHAPTER SEVEN

IMMEDIATELY Kirby had left the house the next morning Melanie stormed down the hall from the office and into the kitchen where Alix was tidying up after breakfast.

'When you left us to dance in peace last night I thought you might have finally been coming to your senses,' she jeered arrogantly. 'But you couldn't let it go at that, could you? You just have to blackmail Kirby into staying by your side for the rest of the evening.'

Alix glanced up from loading the dishwasher, her eyes wide and artless. 'Goodness, I didn't have to force Kirby to stay with me, Melly, it was all his own idea. Perhaps you came on too sickly sweet and he felt the need for a change to take the cloying taste away.'

'Kirby does not find me cloying!' The dispute was hotly given. 'He likes me exactly the way I am. He said so.'

'Then it's strange he didn't choose to spend more time with you, isn't it?'

'Don't worry, he would have—if you hadn't made it impossible!'

Alix burst out laughing. 'You credit me with powers I assure you I don't have, Melly,' she chuckled. 'If my husband had wanted to be with you I'm positive nothing I could have said would have made him alter his decision.'

'Don't give me that! You must have promised him something,' Melanie snapped suspiciously. 'Why else would he have kissed you like he did?'

Now they were getting down to the nitty gritty, Alix smiled. Melanie's confidence had apparently been struck a low blow by that proprietorial demonstration.

'What's wrong, Melly, aren't you so sure of your hold on him any more? And you not even married to him yet,' she made a mockingly sympathetic clicking with her tongue. 'Have you only just realised yours aren't the only covetous eyes that follow my husband around?'

Melanie flushed a dark red, confirming Alix's taunt, but that didn't stop her from blustering, 'Stop calling him that! He hasn't been your husband for years.'

'Oh, but I have a finger full of rings which says he is,' Alix goaded, waving her left hand under the other girl's nose.

'I'm surprised you've got the gall to still wear them.'

Alix's smile was innocent. 'But I wasn't ... until Kirby insisted.'

'And why would he do that?' Melanie snorted.

If she had to ask a question like that then she obviously didn't know Kirby as well as she thought she did, Alix mused in some surprise. But as she had absolutely no intention of enlightening Melanie with the true facts she merely replied guilelessly,

'I think it was because he wanted everyone to know we still belonged together.' Which wasn't quite the way of it, but it was enough to have Melanie turning apoplectic with rage.

'That's a lie!' she screamed shrilly. 'He couldn't possibly want anything to do with you after the hell you made of his life last time. He'll never forgive you for walking out on him like you did, never!'

'Then you have nothing to worry about, have you?' Alix gibed from between stiff lips. She couldn't imagine Kirby forgiving or forgetting either.

Melanie appeared a little mollified by the thought. 'Of course not,' she smirked, trying to recapture her former confidence. 'He's probably only being nice to you in order to get the divorce through more quickly. Heaven only knows why you don't accept the inevitable and go back to Canberra anyway. You've recovered now and there's nothing to keep you here. We'll all be glad to see you leave.'

'*Melanie!* That's an unforgivable thing to say!' Unbeknown to her daughter Clara had entered the room in time to hear the last of her diatribe and her shocked voice had Melanie swinging around guiltily.

'Well, it's true,' she spluttered. 'Even you said she wasn't good enough for Kirby.'

'That was before,' Clara answered calmly.

'So what's different now?'

Clara drew herself up to her full height angrily. 'Quite a number of things, although not the fact that you still happen to be only an employee in this house, the same as I am, and as such you have no right to talk to your employer's wife in such a fashion!'

'You've got to be joking!' Melanie laughed derisively. 'I'll talk to her any way I damned well please. I'm not bowing and scraping to her just because Kirby made the mistake of marrying her. I've been in this house a lot more years than she has.'

'That still doesn't make you the mistress of it!'

'I was as good as, though . . . until *she* came back!' Melanie retaliated bitterly before flouncing through the doorway.

Clara looked across at Alix regretfully. 'I do apologise for that outburst,' she sighed. 'It's true that Melanie has been more or less in charge since you left, but that's still no excuse for her behaviour.'

'It's all right, Clara, I understand,' Alix spoke gently. Over the weeks she had come to greatly appreciate the older woman's friendship. 'We all say things at times that would be better unsaid.'

'But I had no idea she felt so resentful about your return.'

'Yes, well . . .' Alix was still reluctant to discuss the reason behind Melanie's bitterness with her mother. 'I suppose it would be hard to find yourself displaced on such short notice,' she offered extenuatingly.

'Maybe so, maybe so,' Clara conceded heavily. 'But if Kirby's attention to you last night is any guide, then I figure she might have to get used to it.'

'I doubt it,' Alix half laughed, painfully. 'That was only for show, his feelings haven't changed.' And they

were just about back to normal this morning, she
added silently. Actually, she had been surprised he
hadn't reverted last night because she certainly gave
him cause with her constant provocations and unco-
operativeness.

'Oh, I am sorry,' Clara now sympathised, shaking
her head sadly. 'I was hoping you'd been able to patch
up your differences.'

'No, they're as wide as ever. Besides . . .' Alix thrust
her hands into the back pockets of her jeans and
stared moodily down at the floor, 'Kirby's not interested in closing them anyway.'

'You are, though, aren't you, Alix?' softly quizzi-
cal.

'For all the good it will do me,' she shrugged,
knowing that whatever she told Clara would go no
further than that room. They had shared a surprising
number of confidences since the day they had come
to understand each other better. 'Maybe I should go
home, as Melanie suggested, and try to put him out of
my mind like before.'

'Do you think you'll be able to . . . a second time?'

'Probably not, but I've got to start some time.' She
dragged up a lopsided grin and quoted, '*The end is
nigh*—as those people like to print on their gloomy
little prediction boards.'

'The longer you stay the more chance you would
have of changing his mind,' Clara pointed out
shrewdly.

Alix shook her head ruefully. 'If I thought it would

work I might even consider giving it a go, but unfortunately I know the outcome already. Kirby's made his plans and I don't enter into them.'

There wasn't much else to be said on the matter, but during the next few days Alix's thoughts kept returning to their conversation and one evening after dinner she reluctantly opened the subject with Kirby.

'I've been thinking it was time I went home,' she began hesitantly, watching for his reaction over the rim of her cup as they had coffee in the sitting room. And because she didn't have enough of her own money left to pay for a commercial flight was forced to ask, 'Would it be possible for you to fly me back some time in the next week or so?'

Although Kirby's eyes locked with hers it was impossible for Alix to tell what he was thinking. 'Sorry,' he shook his head dispassionately, 'but we're coming into another busy period. You'll have to wait a while longer, I'm afraid.'

Was he being deliberately difficult? Alix wasn't sure and, as a result, her counter-charge was a little on the tentative side.

'But I thought you'd passed your busy period,' she frowned. 'All your cane has been cut, hasn't it?'

'No, we still have the late maturing crop to go,' he relayed offhandedly, and Alix thought he meant to leave it at that, but to her surprise he went on to explain, 'As cane needs to be harvested very quickly once it matures in order to keep the sugar content high, it's necessary to grow varieties which mature early, mid, and late in the season, otherwise it can't all be processed by the mill quickly enough.'

So it was possible he wasn't just being obstructive after all, Alix was forced to concede, and watched covertly as he abruptly left his chair and paced to the windows, watching the assortment of flying insects fluttering against the gauze in their efforts to reach the light inside.

'Why the sudden desire to return home? Is it becoming a bore again?' he drawled sardonically over his shoulder.

'No,' she protested sharply, irritated by his assumption. 'I just didn't want to overstay my welcome.'

He half turned to face her, his expression obscured as he bent his head to apply a light to the tip of his cigarette. 'Has anyone suggested you might be?'

'Only lovable little Melly,' she revealed caustically.

Kirby drew deeply on his cigarette and then viewed the exhaled smoke climbing towards the ceiling. 'Because she took exception to your inference that I didn't spend more time with her at Simon's party as I couldn't stand her company and preferred yours?' he asked grimly.

In order to give herself time to regain control of her escalating temper, Alix replaced her cup and saucer on the small table in front of her and then sat back in her chair, crossing her legs elegantly before replying.

'My, my, but she's a regular little courier pigeon,

isn't she? Is there anything I say that she doesn't twist to suit her own purposes before running to tell you, I wonder?' she queried, angrily flippant. 'However, if you really want the truth, your warped secretary took most exception to my informing her that it was *you* who insisted I wear my wedding and engagement rings. I think she felt you'd failed her very badly when she heard that.'

'What the hell ...!' He bit off the rest of his words and rubbed the back of his neck in exasperation. 'If you've got something to say, then come out and say it, Alix! Don't talk around it in riddles.'

'I *was* saying it, if you only bothered to listen!' she flared, her eyes dark with resentment, her fingers curling tightly against the palms of her hands. 'But it's always been the same ... if Melly says it, then it must be the truth. Not once have you ever taken my word against hers. If she told you I'd grown another head you'd believe her unquestioningly!'

His lips twitched involuntarily. 'But only if she said it was as good to look at as the first,' he advised indolently.

Alix didn't know whether it was the unexpected compliment or her increasing anger which brought tears to her eyes, but either way it didn't stop her from glaring at him, incensed.

'That's right, treat it as a joke! You've already made up your mind, so who cares what I say. I wonder you married me at all believing I was such a chronic liar!' she blazed.

'No one ever said you were a liar, Alix!' He sounded as angry as she was now. 'But even you would have to admit you've had a grudge against Melanie from the day you first arrived here.'

'Oh, so it's a grudge now, is it, that's causing all my troubles? Well, let me tell you something, Kirby Whitman,' she gibed, jumping to her feet and sending him a glance that was almost pitying in its irony. 'If you're looking for someone with an axe to grind I suggest you set your sights in another direction entirely. *I* wasn't the one left still waiting for a proposal four years ago—I'd already received and accepted one!'

'Oh, God, are you back to that again?' His eyes rose skywards in simmering impatience. 'How many times do you have to be told something before you'll admit that you're wrong?'

'Apparently the same number as you, before you'll admit that I'm right,' she retorted, her chin angling higher to conceal the hollowness she felt inside at his continued refusal to believe her. When he still hadn't spoken after a few seconds had elapsed, she sighed despondently and bent to retrieve her cup and saucer, preparing to take them out to the kitchen. 'Anyway, to return to our original discussion,' she began on coming upright again. 'Could you give me some indication as to when you'll have time to fly me home?'

'No, not right at the moment,' he returned tersely, unhelpfully. 'I'll let you know when.'

'Thank you,' she mocked acidly. 'I'll do my best to amuse myself in the meantime.'

'But not with Tim!'

Even without the sharp ring in his tone the words would have been an arbitrary command and Alix's rebellion showed in the blazing blue-green of her eyes. 'If I want to, I shall,' she declared defiantly. 'You're not my keeper, Kirby, just my husband in name only.'

In one fluid movement he was at her side, the taut line of his mouth a clear indication of the rigorous self-control he was exercising as he grasped her wrist and made the cup and saucer rattle dangerously in her hand.

'Don't throw down challenges you can't carry through, Alix,' he warned coldly. 'I have only to remove the keys from all the vehicles and you could very easily discover yourself confined to the property for the remainder of your stay.' A derisive scrutiny of her disgusted expression and he laughed jeeringly, 'A prospect which doesn't exactly enchant you, I see.'

'Did you expect otherwise?' she taunted, breathing hard.

'No, you're still running true to form,' he mocked in return. 'You've never liked it here and you don't bother to conceal the fact.'

It wasn't quite true, but Alix didn't intend to quibble about it now. 'Then why not make time and fly me home as soon as possible?'

Kirby dropped his hand from her wrist and swung away angrily. 'Because it doesn't happen to suit my convenience! I have more to do than cater to your capricious whims and fancies,' he informed her scathingly, heading for the hall. At the door he turned back. 'Just keep in mind what I said about Tim, that's all, or I promise you you'll really have reason to feel sorry for yourself in the not too distant future!'

Alix glared at his departing figure in mounting fury. How dared he think he had the right to tell her who she could see and who she couldn't, and then make threats in an attempt to enforce his petty-minded strictures! If he did refuse her the use of the vehicles then she would arrange for Karen to call and collect her when they planned to go somewhere. One thing was for sure, he wasn't going to get away with treating her like a recalcitrant child with his auto-cratic dictates.

As it happened, Alix and Karen called for her any-way two afternoons later when the members of the Historical Society decided to have a work party sur-vey their newest acquisition, the old cottage they were planning to turn into a museum. Kirby had taken the car himself earlier in the day, leaving her with the choice of an old ute or a Land Rover, neither of which she was familiar with, and as a result she had gone with her friend to view the recent purchase.

Although the property was only on the outskirts of Roslyndale the last owner had led a hermit-like exist-ence until his death some months before and to en-sure his privacy within the twenty-acre boundary had allowed the land to return to an almost virgin state. Now, as Karen carefully followed the car in front along a narrow winding track, made all the more difficult by gnarled root systems protruding above the ground and deep channels carved into the earth by run-off in the wet season, the tropical beauty of the rain-forest began to unfold on either side of them.

Huge ferns and creepers intermingled with a canopy of palms, umbrella trees, hoop-pine, and the tall shaft-like teaks, while as they neared the house sown mangoes, pawpaws and banana plants were easily distinguished. Undergrowth covered the soil like a carpet, even in what had once obviously been a garden but which was now surrounded by a lichen-stained sapling and wire fence which leant at an impossible angle and was only stopped from falling completely by the mass of greenery supporting it. There were fallen leaves and forest debris everywhere, but among the vivid greens there was colour too. Native orchids seemed to cover each mossy rock with their delicate cream, pink, or cyclamen-coloured trails of flowers, and high in the trees above them great clumps of bright yellow spikes clung tenaciously in forked branches.

There wasn't any particular area where it was possible for the four filled vehicles which had made the journey to park and so, following the first driver's lead, Karen pulled off the track as far as she was able and left her car on the outside of the sagging fence.

'What do you think of it?' she asked brightly of Alix once they had alighted and, together with the others, made their way past a permanently dislodged and open wooden gate into the luxuriantly invaded garden.

Alix gazed at the vine-covered cottage considering. A brick chimney at one end had partially collapsed and the iron roof showed great ugly patches of rust. A couple of verandah supports have grown tired of supporting the weight of the pitched roof—many years ago, by Alix's rueful deduction—and their weakening had left the building with a drunken, lopsided air which wasn't improved by the window shutters hanging loosely from the corroded hinges.

'Well, if you wanted it *old*, that's certainly how you got it,' she laughed. 'Do you really think you can restore it to its original condition?'

'Oh, yes,' came the confident reply. 'It's been looked into very thoroughly in that respect and apparently the frame is the main thing, but as that's constructed of red cedar, which is highly resistant to both weather and termites—besides being easy to work and extremely pleasant to look at—it's a good deal more sound than it looks. It's a pity they didn't use the same timber for the verandah supports as well, but I guess we can't have everything,' she grinned wryly. 'The chimney doesn't present much of a problem, the bricks are still lying where they've fallen, so that's just a matter of cleaning them and rebuilding it.'

'And the inside?' One of Alix's brows flicked upwards expressively.

'Yes, well, that is pretty messy,' Karen admitted

with a grin. 'The old feller must have been a hoarder of first class proportions because it's absolutely packed with newspapers dating from goodness knows when, saddles, old china, brassware, and a variety of odds and ends we're all dying to have a look at.'

'Perfect for a Historical Society,' Alix agreed. 'But didn't his relatives want any of it? That sort of thing's becoming very valuable these days.'

Karen shook her head quickly. 'Luckily for us there were no relatives, and as no one else was interested in the place we were allowed to buy it as is, memorabilia included. Now you know why we've been so anxiously awaiting the sale to be finalised. There could be all sorts of local records, etcetera, hidden away in there.'

'He'd lived here for some time, then?'

'You could say that—he was born here,' Karen laughed. 'One of the last true colonials, being born before the six separate Australian colonies became federated States in 1901. He married when he was still fairly young, I believe, but his wife died only a year or so later and he lived here with his parents until they died and then on his own for the last thirty-odd years.'

Ducking beneath the drooping roof, Alix stepped on to the verandah. 'He must have been very lonely,' she speculated.

'Mmm, I suppose so, although it was by choice that he lived in such seclusion, so I guess he must have preferred it that way.'

Alix nodded and followed Karen through the front door into a small vestibule which then led through an ornately designed timber arch into the sitting room, though it seemed doubtful anyone could have sat in the room for a good many years as every available seat had been piled high with books, newspapers, boxes, and a variety of old clothing. Hooks had been driven into the walls and hung with decaying riding tack and the twin glass-bowled lamps sitting on a dust-laden writing desk had obviously been made for use with kerosene.

The two bedrooms hadn't fared much better with regard to orderliness, although one did appear somewhat less congested than the other, but both were fitted with delightful brass bedstands, massive carved oak wardrobes and dressers, and accompanied by inlaid washstand cabinets with tall water pitchers.

Only the kitchen remained to be inspected inside the house and the room was a shambles, with bent and twisted pieces of corrugated iron having been nailed haphazardly across the gaping hole left by the fallen chimney; a giant soot-encrusted wood stove dominating the bottom half of the wall; old and broken pieces of crockery strewn everywhere; cutlery, tin pans, and a large black cauldron lying on the solid timber table; and newspapers, stacks of them, in every conceivable corner.

'It seems that Meg and Irene and a few of the others are going to make a start in here, Joan and Sharon are doing one of the bedrooms, so where do you reckon we ought to try ... at the front?' enquired Karen when their inspection was completed.

'Okay by me,' Alix assented easily as they made their way back through the house. 'What do we do first? Sort through everything to see what's here and then dispose of the rubbish?'

'That's about it to start with,' Karen grimaced. 'At least it will tidy it up somewhat so we can see what we're doing later.'

Beginning at the top of the pile of boxes resting on an old chaise-longue, the two girls were soon engrossed in picking through items as diverse as recent newspapers, rusted machinery parts, unused lamp wicks, empty boot polish tins, and a selection of bone china ornaments, some of which were broken and some still intact. The next box proved just as interesting, but when they came across some papers of a much older vintage they found themselves compulsively stopping to read a few of the articles.

'There'll be plenty of time for that later.' A large hand was suddenly placed over the printing which had captured Alix's attention. 'You're supposed to be classifying, not reading, you know.'

With a slightly guilty laugh she brought her thoughts back to the present, folded the paper carefully, and looked up with a grin. 'Hello, Tim. I didn't think you were coming today.'

'Neither did I originally, but young Peter said he'd be able to manage without me for the afternoon, so I thought I'd come along and lend a hand.' He ran his eyes ruefully around the cramped room. 'There's certainly a lot that needs to be done, isn't there?'

'You can say that again,' chirped Karen in heartfelt agreement. 'It's going to take weeks to plough through all these.'

'And even longer if you keep stopping for a read,' he teased. Then, to Alix, 'I half expected Kirby to be here this afternoon as well, but I don't see his car outside.'

Alix shook her head. 'No, he had to go into town this morning on business and because he also has a meeting of the co-operative tonight he decided to make a day of it,' she explained.

Tim clicked his fingers in a gesture of recollection. 'That's right, the meeting! Dad did mention in at breakfast this morning, but I'd forgotten all about it. Well, rather than have dinner all on your own why not come home with us and eat at our place when we've finished here?' he invited casually. 'I can drive you back to Maiyatta afterwards.'

Momentarily, Kirby's last warning sprang to mind, but Alix determinedly paid it no heed. Why should she eat dinner on her own when she could enjoy it in good company?

'Thank you, that would be very nice,' she accepted with a smile. 'Provided it's okay with your mother, of course. She won't be expecting me and I wouldn't like to put her to any trouble.'

'No worries there,' Karen advised, grinning. 'Mum always cooks as if preparing for a battalion. One more mouth to feed means nothing.'

Once Tim had left to add to the numbers of men engaged in shoring up the wall of the kitchen so they could dismantle the rest of the chimney prior to cleaning the bricks and rebuilding it, Alix and Karen turned their attention to the boxes still remaining to be checked. There were about twenty in all, but after completing only another three they decided on a change and began sifting through the various piles of clothing scattered indiscriminately about the room.

One heap of threadbare working shirts and pants in the corner proved to conceal an old camphorwood chest and on levering open the clasp the girls gasped with delight. It was packed to the brim with ladies' dresses, shawls, petticoats, hose, handkerchiefs, and even a pair of most uncomfortable looking stays, but which had all been lovingly folded between sheets of tissue interspersed with hand-made muslin lavender bags.

'I wonder who they belonged to?' Karen breathed excitedly, withdrawing a lace-trimmed fine lawn petticoat and holding it cautiously against herself.

'His wife?' Alix suggested as she lightly fingered the perfectly preserved material.

'Probably,' the younger girl nodded. 'It looks like it was a woman's hand that packed them, and that could have been his mother ... some time after his wife died.'

'Mmm, sounds feasible. Oh, look at this! Isn't it beautiful?' Alix exclaimed suddenly, and opened an intricately painted Chinese wood and paper parasol which she twisted gently over one shoulder.

'Shouldn't we tell the others what we've uncovered?'

Karen grinned conspiratorially. 'Not just yet, let's look a little bit further first. Then we can all have a "Look what we've found!" session at the end.'

And that was just what it turned out to be, for every room had something of interest in an historical sense. Even the derelict outbuildings provided their share with two old sulkies being unearthed in one and a number of square, iron ship's containers that had been used as water tanks in another. The only discovery to tarnish their general pleasure was the chance sighting of a disturbed taipan by two of the men as they checked through the sheds, and although they had all been aware of such a likelihood with the place so overgrown and with so many piles of scrap material lying around to make perfect habitats for them, it was a sobering event all the same. As they rarely came south of the border into New South Wales, and certainly never ventured as far as the Capital Territory, Alix looked askance at Karen and Tim when they were told the news.

'Are they really the world's deadliest snake?' she queried apprehensively.

'So they reckon,' Karen shrugged, leaving Tim to advise, 'The King Cobra is reputed to be deadlier, but only if he's fully grown. Either way, I doubt whether it matters much if you were bitten by one or the other. Deadly is *deadly*, as far as I'm concerned.'

Alix wrinkled her nose in distaste. 'Do you often come across them?'

'Not really,' he tried to reassure her, but still couldn't suppress a grin at her obvious aversion. 'Like most snakes they're very shy and would prefer to keep out of your way if they can.'

'And if they can't?' She eyed him sidelong.

'Then I guess you could say you've got trouble because they're an extremely ferocious species. Rather than biting once and then slithering away, they'll strike repeatedly at a foe, and stand while they're doing it too, I'm afraid.'

'Stand? What do you mean *stand*?' she gulped.

'He means they don't have any qualms about rearing up and attacking you as high as the waist, instead of in a handy place like a foot or an ankle,' Karen grimaced.

'Oh, lovely!' Alix couldn't repress an involuntary shudder.

'I'd still rather have them than spiders,' Karen went on fervently. 'At least a snake will make an effort to avoid you . . . spiders don't!'

'Personally, I'm not a fan of either of them. They both make me feel cold all over,' Alix pulled a rueful face, and purposely changed the subject before she started imagining every chance movement she saw was a snake or a spider on the prowl.

It was almost dark by the time they all managed to get away from the house, which looked a great deal more tidy now but no less full, as there was still the double-checking to be done before they could actually dispose of anything. The iron had been tem-

porarily returned to the kitchen wall and sheets of
heavy duty plastic laid over the worst of the holes in
the roof to prevent deterioration to the inside in case
of rain.

'Well, it was certainly a novel way to spend an
afternoon,' Alix commented as they began weaving
their way out through the rain forest. 'I wouldn't have
believed it possible for one person to collect such an
amount of litter. I've never seen so many newspapers
together at one time in my life! He certainly had a
thing about them, didn't he?'

'And how!' Karen laughed. 'I'll have to check with
the *Mail's* offices in town to see if they have copies of
every issue. Their premises were completely gutted by
fire many years ago and they might like to copy some
of them if they haven't a full set, because these do go
back a long way. So far the oldest I've come across
has been 1912. How about you?'

'1910, although it wasn't a local *Mail*, it was another paper. Somebody or other's *Gazette*, I think.'

'The *Miners' Gazette*?'

'Mmm, it could have been,' Alix allowed thoughtfully. 'Why, do you know it?'

Karen nodded quickly, unable to take her eyes
from the track because it was a particularly difficult
section they were traversing. 'Oh, yes, it was a
flourishing paper late last century when the goldfields
were booming up this way, although I hadn't realised
it lasted under that name for so long after the mining
petered out. It changed hands quite a few times—and

names—in the end before it finally ceased production.'

'Well, I reckon the chap who bought it must have read it down a mine, because it was sure dusty and dirty enough,' Alix revealed drily, brushing her hands down the sides of her slacks. 'A shower will be very welcome after sifting through that mess.'

'Coming up shortly,' Karen promised as they eventually turned out of the property and on to the bitumen highway where she was immediately able to increase speed. 'We'll stop at your place so you can change and then head for home and dinner, okay?'

Alix's pleased expression mirrored her thoughts. 'Sounds delightful,' she breathed eloquently.

CHAPTER EIGHT

'THEY must have had quite a lot on the agenda for the meeting, Kirby's not home yet,' Tim indicated the empty garage as he drove Alix up to the house later that evening.

Alix smothered a relieved sigh but didn't comment. Although the hour wasn't late she had been on tenterhooks all night lest there had been a confrontation between Kirby and Tim when he brought her home. She was finding that spoken defiance was one thing, but it was another matter entirely when it came to putting it into action, and especially where her husband was concerned! Luckily, though, she could now relax a little, and she smiled gratefully at her companion as he walked around the car to open the door for her.

'Thanks very much, Tim, it was good of you to bring me back, and of your mother to have me. It was far more pleasant than eating alone.'

'You're welcome any time,' he advised sincerely, grey eyes twinkling. 'Even if your husband's too blind to appreciate you, others aren't.'

'Oh, well . . .' she laughed nervously. It wasn't the type of conversation she wanted to develop. 'There's two sides to every argument, you know, so he no doubt considers he has cause.'

Tim placed his hand beneath her elbow and escorted her to the top of the steps. 'I still think he's a shortsighted fool,' he smiled wryly, then dropped his voice to murmur, 'Because if you're not still in love with him then I'm a poor judge.'

'Th-that's ridiculous!' Alix protested hollowly, attempting to disguise her initial look of shocked dismay at his perception. 'We're getting divorced.'

'Which doesn't alter the facts in the slightest,' he declared softly, and tilted her wary face up to his. 'I've been friends with Kirby ever since he arrived in this district and I applaud his choice of a wife, so if you ever need any help from someone who would like to be friends with you both, you know where to come, hmm?'

Alix expelled a tremulous breath, her gratitude evident in her shining eyes. 'I'll remember,' she whispered throatily. 'And thank you ... for everything.'

He lifted a discounting hand and smiled his understanding. 'As I said before, you're welcome ... any time.'

Having watched him drive away Alix switched on the hall light and walked slowly into the house, running a hand around the back of her neck to allow a breath of air to reach her nape. It was oppressively hot for an early spring evening and she started for the kitchen to get herself a cold drink and then, impulsively changing her mind, headed for the bathroom instead. Another shower would be more cooling than a drink.

When she turned it on the water stung her heated skin like icy needles, but she refused to add any hot to the rushing stream and stood relishing every minute of it. Finally, after having reluctantly decided she couldn't stay there all night, she turned the water off, patted herself dry, and wrapped the towel sarong-wise around her slender form. Her bedroom was only just across the hall and she hadn't bothered to collect her housecoat beforehand as she had been anxious to sample the refreshing cascade.

She turned the hall light off before entering her room and switching on her own light, but immediately she did so she came to a shocked standstill at the sight which met her disbelieving eyes. Kirby was stretched out on her bed, hands clasped loosely behind his head, a pair of navy blue hip-hugging shorts his only covering.

'But—but the car ...' Alix said the first thing that came into her head, waving a hand vaguely in the direction of the empty garage. 'It's not outside.'

Kirby fixed her with a glare of such glittering intentness that she felt her insides begin to quake. 'I left it in town for some panel-beating to be done. It seems one of the doors has recently managed to get itself pushed in.'

Oh, was that what had put the steely ring in his tone? Alix was thankful it wasn't anything else and rushed into a placatory explanation.

'I'm sorry, I did mean to tell you, but it must have slipped my mind,' she attempted a wryly apologetic half smile. They hadn't been talking at the time, actually. 'It really wasn't my fault, though. I came out of the supermarket the last time I was in town and found it like that. Someone must have backed into it, or something, I guess.'

Kirby didn't appear particularly interested, going on instead to bite out satirically, 'Well, here's something else for you to guess at! Who do you think gave me a lift home tonight?'

'How should I know?' Her eyes rounded in astonishment.

'Then allow me to tell you.' He swung his legs over the side of the bed and came to his feet in a rolling motion which reminded Alix of a towering wave about to crush all before it. 'It was Norman Acton. You *do* know Norm, don't you?'

Of course! He and his wife, Meg, had been out at the cottage with them all afternoon. He was a nice enough man but not exactly what one would call bright. She nodded her acknowledgment of the question.

'And shall I also tell you who he informed me he had met this afternoon?'

Alix chewed apprehensively at her lip and watched nervously as he paced menacingly closer, her assenting, 'If you want to,' barely above a whisper.

'Oh, I want to all right!' he snarled. 'He met Tim Aylward's young wife, that's who! "A pretty girl with big blue eyes and lovely blonde hair",' was the mimicking narration as a snaking hand twined roughly within that very same blonde hair. 'It seems you've been promoted from his girl-friend to his wife now!'

The garrulous, senseless, old fool! Alix cursed inwardly. Why, oh, why couldn't he have listened properly to her name when they had been introduced?

'But—but I hardly saw Tim all afternoon. We were all working together at the cottage. That's just some stupid misconception Norm's thought up by himself,' she cried, trying to prise free of his hold.

Kirby wasn't about to release her, however, and his grip tightened remorselessly. 'Not one you're ever likely to disprove, though, since you apparently never go anywhere without him!'

'That's not true! I didn't know Tim was even going to be there today. He said originally that he expected to be too busy to come.'

'But he made a magnificent sacrifice and came anyway!' he countered sarcastically.

'Well, that's not my fault,' she flared. 'I've got no say in where he goes or doesn't go.'

'No, you just provide the attraction! But you do control where you go, don't you, Alix?'

She winced at the emphasising tug on her hair which accompanied his words and answered with a wary, 'Y-yes, I suppose so.'

'And you did choose to go out with him tonight, because that *was* who brought you home, wasn't it?' His eyes glinted dangerously.

'So?' She valiantly tried to brazen it out.

Suddenly Alix was free, but only fleetingly, and then she was snatched off her feet in one sweeping movement which took her completely by surprise.

'So I think it's about time you learnt, once and for all, just whose wife you really are!' he seethed with a decided rasp in his voice, making for the bed.

'You wouldn't dare!'

There was no need for Kirby to reply, all the answer Alix needed was in the unyielding blue of his eyes, and with a choked gasp of panic she began to struggle violently, kicking and twisting in an attempt to break the iron bands which bound her to his broad chest.

When this wasn't successful she lashed out with her hand to catch him a stinging blow to the side of his unprotected face but, in retaliation, she was thrown grimly on to the bed to be crushed beneath the weight of his body as his lips came down on hers, savagely demanding, and long fingers loosened her covering towel.

Fighting desperately now, Alix hammered at him with clenched fists, sobbing deep in her throat when it produced no result for an imprisoning grip around her wrists and an uncontrollable flicker of humiliating desire as he cradled a rounded breast in his seeking hand.

'No, Kirby ... *no*!' she at last managed to drag her mouth from his to pant frantically, knowing her strength to be fading. 'You've no right ...'

'No right!' His dusky framed eyes narrowed coldly and he deliberately trailed his fingers over her curving form in a long sensuous caress which set her quivering to his touch. 'I have a legal certificate which says I have every right!' he grated before capturing her trembling lips again in a kiss which jolted her with its fierceness and had her striving wildly once more to escape.

When it came, his final inexorable possession brought no pleasure but only pain and a feeling of utter degradation. It was total subjugation by the dominant male with no thought of desire or passion, let alone love, in the union but merely a propelling anger to prove mastery in the most humbling way possible.

The one redeeming feature in the whole desolating experience for Alix was the knowledge that it obviously hadn't provided Kirby with any satisfaction either. It was evident when he moved away from her to sit on the side of the bed, head lowered, elbows resting on his knees, and the knuckles of his intertwined fingers white with strain.

'I'm sorry,' he apologised heavily, his breathing harsh. 'That was a swine of a thing to have done under the circumstances.'

Alix stared dry-eyed at the tautly hunched shoulders, the hard lump in her throat threatening to deprive her of her voice. 'Rape always is ... under any circumstances,' she condemned bitterly. When a deeply exhaled sigh was his only acknowledgment she huddled miserably beneath the sheltering bed-clothes, aware as never before of the vulnerability of her situation, and proposed shakily, 'Perhaps now you'll be able to find the time to fly me home.'

'No!' Kirby's back straightened as if he had been flicked with a whip, an underlying current of savagery in his tone as he half turned to fix her with an in-flexible gaze. 'I've already explained why it's impossible.'

'Then you won't mind if I keep my door locked from now on?' she attempted to gibe, but her voice was too unsteadily tearful for it to be successful.

'There's no need, I won't come near you again.'

The words were spoken coldly and with such finality that Alix had no doubt he meant them, but what she didn't realise until some weeks had passed was that he intended to abide by them quite so liter-ally.

Apart from their meetings at the breakfast and dinner table, which he kept to the minimum duration, he *didn't* come near her. When he spoke he was polite but so distant he might have been a stranger, and al-though Alix knew she should have been relieved by his cool remoteness, she was anything but. She was restless and introspective, and subject to fits of aching depression even Karen's good humour couldn't dispel.

In her mind she believed Kirby's assault should have killed whatever she felt for him but, to her self-disgust, she knew in her heart that it hadn't. He still had the power to make her incredibly aware of him, to remember the tenderness he was capable of showing and, most distressing of all, to make her long for the once persuasive touch of his lips and the stirring feel of his hands.

A month and a half later Alix received the doctor's confirmation that she was pregnant with an outward calm at complete odds with the despair which churned her insides to a quivering jelly. She had suspected as much, but while there had still been the chance she might have been mistaken she had clung grimly to it. Today her last false hope had been swept unrelentingly away. After wishing for a child for so long in the early days of their marriage she was now expecting one at a time when she least wanted to be. Not that she didn't want Kirby's child—she still wanted that with every fibre of her being—but the consequences if he should discover her pregnancy were frightening and made an early departure on her part imperative.

Never once did she consider he might not want his child, she knew him too well for that, but to her mind that only left him with two choices, neither of which was acceptable to Alix.

He could either revise his decision regarding a divorce, but there was no way she was going to remain married to him as a matter of convenience just because she happened to be the mother of his child. Or else he could go through with the divorce and then press for custody once he was married to Melanie, but there was also no way Alix would ever countenance a child of hers being reared by someone else, and definitely not Melanie!

No, she had to leave immediately, before he ever found out. He wouldn't come after her, she knew that from past experience, but that still didn't solve the problem of just *how* she was going to get away. Certainly, she didn't possess enough money to pay for such a trip, nor could she involve Karen or Tim in her troubles. They would be bound to ask why she wanted to return home suddenly and she seriously doubted her ability to bluff her way through their enquiries because she had no intention of telling anyone the true reason behind her panicking desire to leave. It was no use writing to her mother either to ask for a loan because she knew her parent would immediately become suspicious of the request and Alix couldn't take the chance of her ringing Kirby to find out what was going on.

To soothe her agitated nerves before driving home Alix stopped at a coffee lounge in Roslyndale and ordered a drink, taking her time over it and drawing deeply on a cigarette as she spun the time out. There was nothing to rush back for and it was as good a place as any to try and come up with an answer to her problem. But it wasn't until she despondently walked to the counter to pay for her coffee that one presented itself. On opening her purse she found her eyes drawn irresistibly to the forgotten cheque Kirby had given her in the hospital and which she had steadfastly refused to cash.

Now it was another matter, however, and on

emerging into the sunlight she hurried quickly across the street to the bank and then to the travel agents. It wasn't quite enough to cover the cost of a plane ticket, but it was certainly sufficient to pay her fare on a bus with ample left over for meals on the way. She could meet the coach at eight the next morning and be on her way before anyone knew she had gone, and it really couldn't have been a more opportune day if she had planned it because Kirby, together with Melanie, naturally, would have left long before then themselves as they were flying up to the tablelands for a cattle sale.

All the way home Alix was making mental notes of what she needed to do before leaving. There were her things to be packed secretly, of course, and letters to be written, and all the while pretending that everything was the same as usual. That was going to be the hardest part, she decided—to act as if she expected to see Kirby again when she knew all too well that just wasn't the case.

On reaching her bedroom Alix quickly accomplished her packing, although she took the precaution of locking her door just in case Melanie barged in unannounced as she had on other occasions, but the letters took far longer than she had envisaged. There was a short one for Clara—not too difficult to pen; one each for Karen and Tim—finally achieved after a few attempts; and one for Kirby—a brief, stilted little note which said all the correct things but none of those she wanted to say, and took the remainder of the afternoon to write.

For dinner Alix prepared one of her husband's favourite meals. As a parting gesture of goodwill? she asked herself ruefully, then immediately dismissed the idea as foolish. It would take a whole lot more than a nice meal to generate anything favourable between them now. Yet, despite her resolutions to the contrary, she couldn't steer her gaze away from him during that last meal they would be sharing together. It was as if she was committing each feature and expression to memory, knowing that there was very little likelihood of her ever seeing him again once she left, and that they were going to have to last her a lifetime.

Despair sent burning tears welling into her eyes at the thought and she looked down swiftly at her almost untouched food. How could she ever have believed she had got him out of her system? The pain of loving him would be with her always and her one hope of assuaging it the fulfilment of her desire that the child she carried would be a son to resemble the father she loved so achingly.

'Your plans all set for tomorrow?' Kirby suddenly lifted his head to enquire.

Fear of having been discovered in some unknown way drained the colour from Alix's face leaving it ashen, her eyes wide and staring as they clashed with his. 'Wh-what p-plans?' she stammered nervously.

His upper lip curled with a restrained exasperation. 'There's no need to look scared out of your wits, Alix, I do know you've continued to see Tim. I was referring to your plans for the work out at the cottage.

That is where you'll both be tomorrow, isn't it?'

'Oh ... oh, yes,' she shuddered in relief. 'Along with the others, of course.'

'Of course,' he agreed drily.

'Kirby!' She laid one hand pleadingly on the table. All of a sudden it was terribly important to her that she disabuse him of his ideas regarding Tim and herself. 'Please believe me, I feel nothing for Tim but friendship, the same as he feels for me. There's never been anything between us of a—a romantic nature.'

'Is that so?' His expression said only one thing ... he wasn't convinced. 'Well, never mind, my love, perhaps you'll be able to alter that in time.'

'I don't want to alter it ... I was being honest,' she whispered sadly.

'A true confession?' His eyes slanted tauntingly, then rapidly narrowed as he went on to probe suspiciously, 'but why choose this particular night to be so honest, hmm?'

Oh, God, she had nearly blown it! She was no match for him in a battle of wits, she never had been. In panic she drew up her shoulders in a feigned hunch of ignorance.

'Why not tonight?' she countered lightly.

'Because tonight you not only sound different, you even *look* different in some indefinable way.'

Alix dropped her hands into her lap so he couldn't see her curling fingers. 'You're imagining things,' she made herself laugh.

'Am I?'

'I think so.' She held his penetrating glance valiantly. 'You've conditioned yourself to suspect me no
matter what I say concerning Tim.'

'Maybe you're right.' Kirby ran a hand through his
hair, sighing ruefully, before getting to his feet and
advising, 'Don't bother with coffee for me tonight,
thanks, Alix, I'll make my own in the office. There
are a couple of matters I want to check on before we
leave for the sale tomorrow.'

Alix watched him leave with hungry eyes, collecting more memories to take with her.

Understandably, her sleep was disturbed and fitful
that night. She knew she couldn't stay, but it was
breaking her heart to leave, and by the time the sun
appeared on the eastern horizon her eyes were red
from having cried herself back to sleep so many
times. From her room it was possible to hear Kirby
moving about the house as he prepared for his trip
but, although she was already dressed, Alix didn't
venture out. For one thing her eyes would have
caused suspicion, and if they hadn't then she was
positive her strained manner would have done. She
did, however, watch his tall drill-clad figure through
the curtains as he headed for the ute and climbed in,
but she didn't see him drive away. Her eyes were so
full of tears again it was impossible for her to see anything at all.

Prior to leaving the house she placed Clara's letter
in a prominent position on one of the kitchen cup-
boards and Kirby's on the pillow of his bed. He slept

in a different room now from the one they had shared. Probably because he didn't want to be reminded of her, Alix deduced miserably. Karen and Tim's letters she planned to post in town while she waited for the bus. There would be plenty of time to drop them in the mailbox because they were already stamped and she intended to arrive long before anyone who might recognise her was on the road. She didn't want to start any speculation before she had even left Rosyln-dale.

At that hour of the day, with no cane trucks yet to avoid, it was a very fast journey to the coast and she left the car parked out of sight behind the bank, as she had advised Kirby in his note she would be doing, and from there carried her luggage to the bus depot. Her watch said eight o'clock exactly when the air-conditioned coach pulled in and, handing her ticket to the driver, Alix took her seat with mixed feelings —relief at having made her flight without discovery, and regret that she had been forced to leave in the same secretive fashion as last time. God only knew what Kirby would think of her when he returned and found she had walked out for a second time!

The journey was pleasant enough, Alix supposed, and although the coach was very comfortable, the other passengers friendly, and the tinted windows made viewing the beautiful coastal scenery very easy on the eyes, by the time they reached Townsville for lunch she was already wondering how she was going to survive the enforced inactivity for another two and a half days.

Her purchase of a couple of books and magazines helped pass some of the afternoon hours, but she was still anxiously awaiting a chance to stretch her legs when they arrived at their dinner stop in Proserpine— a well known departure point for tourists visiting the Whitsunday Islands on the Reef—and she was one of the first off the bus into the fading afternoon sunshine.

Exchanging a remark with the affable driver, she looked about her interestedly, her gaze being drawn to a man who leant negligently against a wooden awning support in front of the café, his head angled downwards as he lit a cigarette. He was dressed much the same as Kirby had been when she last saw him— the same fawn drills, the same broad-brimmed hat pulled down to shade his face—and she looked away quickly, a heavy ache settling in the region of her heart. Had he returned and found her letter yet? she wondered.

When her glance involuntarily travelled back the stockman's way again it was to find he had moved. He was walking towards them, in fact, but when he raised his head and the sun slashed across his commanding features Alix felt her legs grow weak as she stared in shocked recognition and, for the second time in her life, her husband was pinpointed at the end of a long diminishing tunnel as a black haze overwhelmed her vision and she passed out.

This time when she opened her eyes again it was in totally alien surroundings. A swift darting survey had her guessing it to be a hotel bedroom where she was resting on the flower-patterned quilt of a large double bed, while overhead a ceiling fan revolved gently through the air. Of Kirby there was no sign and, frowning as she slipped her feet to the floor, she began to wonder if it hadn't been her imagination playing cruel tricks on her, after all.

'How are you feeling?'

The familiar voice came from the direction of the doors which opened on to the balcony and Alix knew her sight hadn't deceived her. It had been Kirby's electrifying blue gaze which collided with hers at the bus stop.

'Okay, I guess,' she shrugged, and reached for the glass carafe beside the bed to pour herself some cold water. 'I'm sorry I fainted like that, but you were the last person I expected to see.'

'So I gathered.' The curving line of his attractive mouth pulled upwards wryly as he leisurely made his way into the room. 'By the way, you don't happen to have a set of keys that doesn't belong to you in your bag, do you?'

'A set of keys?' Alix couldn't have been more astounded by the question if he had asked her if she could fly.

'Mmm, for the car you used this morning. You considerately locked it, but we couldn't find the keys,' he elaborated in a slow drawl.

'Oh, I—I'm so sorry,' she murmured awkwardly, creamy-skinned cheeks flushing rosily with embarrassment at her own stupidity as she delved into the bag which had been left on the end of the bed. Had she really locked it and then automatically retained the keys? Finding them in one of the side compartments, she held them out to him, her cheeks reddening anew. 'I really am sorry, but—but you needn't have come after me for them, I would have posted them to you when I realised what I'd done. You *have* got a spare you could have used in the meantime, haven't you?'

'Fortunately.'

So if it wasn't for the keys, why was he here? Alix neither wanted to ask, nor to stay and find out, and gaining her feet she closed her bag with a snap and eyed him considerably less confidently than she would have liked.

'Well then, I think perhaps I'd better be rejoining the coach party,' she suggested restively. 'I wouldn't want them to leave without me.'

'They will, though, all the same,' he advised calmly. 'You see, I happen to have cancelled your ticket, *Miss* Ingram.'

'You did *what*?' She stared at him in dismay until an increasing anger obliterated her nervousness. 'Then you can damn well un-cancel it again, can't you? You've got no right whatsoever to interfere with my arrangements, Kirby. I want to go home—I *am* going home—and I'll travel under any name I choose while I'm about it!'

'But not while you're still my *wife* and you're carrying *my* child!'

His words struck at Alix with such biting force that

she collapsed on to the edge of the bed again, crushed, the rapid pounding against her ribs a sign of her inner agitation. There wasn't much use denying it. This was obviously the reason for his appearance.

'But—but how . . . ?' she started to stammer.

Kirby's glance narrowed a little contemptuously. 'You really should have known better, my love, than to expect to keep something like that a secret in a small country town. I ran into Robert Miles while I was in town this morning,' the doctor! Alix recalled with a sinking feeling, 'and not surprisingly, all things considered, he offered me his congratulations.'

Alix chewed at her lower lip miserably. 'And what did you say?'

'What in hell do you think I said?' The livid expression on his face as he strode closer had her defensively backing further on to the bed. 'I asked him what he was talking about, of course! Whereupon he explained, and then promptly apologised for stealing my wife's thunder. Wasn't that considerate of him?' he gibed. 'More considerate than my selfish bloody wife who skips town in order to hide it from me, that's for sure!'

Sensing what was coming, Alix gathered all her courage and shook her head in denial. 'I'm not going back with you, Kirby,' she breathed tremulously.

'Be damned you're not! You're coming with me right now,' he rapped peremptorily, leaning forward to grip one of her arms. 'We can pick up your luggage from the lobby on the way.'

'No!' With unexpected strength she knocked his hand away and sprang to her feet. 'I'm not going with you ... I'm going home,' she asserted determinedly and, hoping to catch him off balance, whirled for the door.

How he made it before her she never knew, but his fingers were in control of the door handle long before hers reached it.

'Maiyatta's your home from now on, Alix, and whether you like it or not that's where we're going,' he told her adamantly.

'Just so you can pretend to all your friends that we're one big happy family and that your wife hasn't really walked out on you twice?'

'No, damn it!' His eyes blazed into hers fiercely. 'Because I must be the world's prize fool. I happen to want my stubborn, exasperating wife back!'

'And when did you decide that?' Alix demanded scornfully, backing away. 'When the doctor told you I was pregnant?'

Kirby slowly stalked after her, his eyes never wavering from her guarded face. 'No, it was the day I saw a pale little wraith in hospital in Canberra. I knew then that I'd only been kidding myself into thinking I could do without you.'

'I don't believe you,' she shook her head wildly, fearfully. She wanted to believe what she heard, but she just couldn't. 'You're only saying that because you want the baby. You would have said something before this otherwise. You and Melanie have. . . .'

'Melanie resigned this morning.'

Melanie resigned! Her mind refused to take it all in. He wasn't saying anything she had expected to hear and when she found herself with the wall at her back and nowhere left to retreat to her eyes sought his face desperately, apprehensively, as his hands came to rest on the wall on either side of her head, his wide shoulders blocking out the rest of the room as he bent towards her.

Gradually, tentatively almost, his dark head closed with hers and his tantalising mouth began a feather-light exploration of her trembling and parted lips. 'I love you, Alix, I always have and I always will,' he groaned huskily against their soft sweetness. 'Believe me, I was making arrangements to come after you long before Robert told me about the baby.'

Alix couldn't think straight. The tempting pressure was throwing her emotions into a turmoil and turning her thoughts incoherent, as always. She wanted to respond, her body was clamouring for her to do so, but still she was unsure of him. In the end, when she could refuse the tormenting demand of her own desire no longer, she accepted a compromise.

'If you're lying, please, oh, please don't ever let me find out,' she begged against the roving lips which were setting her senses on fire.

CHAPTER NINE

KIRBY caught her to him possessively and as his kisses changed from a provocative enticement to a passionate ardour Alix temporarily, but willingly, relinquished all her uncertainties and arched against him with pliant fervour, her hands tangling in his curly hair, her lips moving invitingly beneath his.

His experienced lovemaking had always been able to arouse her emotions unbelievably, and this time was no exception. Or perhaps it was even greater. There was a driving need to assure, and in turn be reassured, that her love wasn't misplaced, and she gave herself up to his exciting caresses uninhibitedly, making no demur on this occasion when he swung her into his arms and swiftly carried her to the bed. In a warm haze of ecstasy she took as much pleasure in rediscovering the delights of his virile body as he did in hers, and when their exploding desires could be contained no longer their joining into a single rapturous entity lifted her to the blissful, soaring heights of heaven.

Later, after settling her into the crook of his arm beneath the single covering sheet, her head lying against his warm bronzed shoulder, Kirby brushed her tousled hair back from her forehead with gentle fingers.

'I meant what I said, Alix,' he murmured deeply, the blue of his eyes as clear as the sea on a summer's day. 'I love you more than you'll ever know.'

'Oh, Kirby!' Her voice shook with the force of her feelings. She wanted so much to believe him, she needed to believe him, but there were so many questions still unanswered that not even now, as he held her so close to him, could she quite bring herself to that completely undoubting state. 'I want to believe you, but I—I'm sorry, I just can't!' she revealed sadly. 'So many words have been spoken which point to the reverse.'

'I know, love, I know,' he soothed. 'I should never have allowed my pride to dictate responses designed to deliberately give that impression.'

Alix evaded his rueful gaze and concentrated on the rhythmic rise and fall of his chest instead. 'I did that to you too sometimes,' she admitted guiltily. 'I guess my efforts must have been very transparent, though, because you certainly acted as if you knew what my reaction would be when you kissed me over there,' waving a hand towards the other side of the room.

'I guessed . . . I hoped!' He tilted her pensive face up to his to kiss her lips softly. 'Your appeal for me to believe that Tim meant nothing to you set me thinking very deeply last night because I couldn't uncover a reason for it until I found you'd left this morning. Then I figured it must have been your way of leaving with a clean slate and I hoped—prayed is probably closer to the truth—that meant you still felt something for me. If you hadn't, I couldn't see why you would have bothered to explain about you and Tim. I reckoned you wouldn't have cared what I thought if there were no feelings there at all.'

'Oh, there were feelings there all right,' she smiled wistfully. 'I cried so much last night at the thought of never seeing you again I had to soak my eyes with cold pads this morning to take the redness out before I dared show my face outside.'

'It would have saved a lot of worry and heartache on both sides then if I'd seen Robert yesterday instead of today.' His eyes searched hers intently. 'Why did you leave, Alix? Didn't you think I'd want the child ... or were you worried I might think it was Tim's?'

For a moment a surprised expression overcame her thoughtful features. 'Strangely, that never once occurred to me—that you might think it was Tim's—I suppose I should have done considering how you felt about our friendship, but I didn't, I took it for granted you would know it was yours.' Abruptly she pushed herself up on one elbow to question urgently, 'You *don't* think the baby is Tim's, do you, Kirby?'

'I wouldn't be here if I did,' he divulged wryly.

Alix subsided against him again, her sudden fear allayed. 'As for the other—well, I guess I knew right from the start that you would want it. I'm not completely ignorant regarding my husband's character, you know,' she half smiled.

'Then why leave?'

'I didn't know what you would do when you found out about it,' she confessed throatily, still uncertain even now.

'What I would do!' A frown settled on his forehead and he stared at her quizzically. 'What on earth did you expect me to do that was so terrible you felt you had to run away to avoid it?'

'I couldn't bear the thought of only being accepted in your house because you'd mistakenly made me pregnant, or—or ...' Tears started into her eyes and it was impossible for her to voice her deepest anxieties.

'Or ... what?' Kirby prompted, his tone roughening. 'Don't stop now, Alix. I think this discussion is long overdue and it's time you and I set the record straight for all time.'

Alix wiped her fingers across her wet cheeks, nodding, and continued falteringly, 'I thought you—you might try and take the b-baby away from me after the divorce and—and then you'd marry Melanie and I —I'd never see it again.'

'Oh, God!' he groaned, and clasped her to him convulsively. 'I never even contemplated divorcing you, my love, and I've certainly never experienced the slightest desire to marry Melanie. I already have the only wife I've ever wanted ... I just can't seem to keep her, that's all,' ironically.

'But you said you intended getting a divorce the day you brought me back, and—and Melanie knew about it too. Not long after you walked out of the room she couldn't wait to tell me what you were planning to do,' she accused.

'How could she?' he asked, amazed. 'I only invented the idea because you flung that damned suggestion at me as I was leaving.'

Alix couldn't entirely submerge her suspicion and it showed in her doubting eyes. 'But you must have told her. How else would she have known?'

Kirby's mouth levelled furiously. 'By eavesdropping! It's the only logical explanation.'

It was possible, Alix had to acknowledge. In fact, it was just the sort of behaviour she would expect from Melanie, but there was more to it than that.

'Even if she did, you still denounced *me* as being jealous and spiteful because I threatened to hold up your plans,' she reminded him reproachfully. 'What else was I to think but that you were in a hurry to marry her?'

'I wasn't referring to my plans when I said that, you little idiot,' he smiled down at her lazily. 'I was referring to your threat to name her as co-respondent. You were always charging me with having an affair with her and it made me see red every time you did it.' He traced the outline of her soft lips with a forefinger, his eyes dark and serious. 'I've never been unfaithful to you, Alix. If I couldn't have you, I didn't want anyone else.'

'Melanie said you did,' she sighed dolefully.

'It appears there's been quite a few things Melanie

has said that I know nothing about. Happily though, that doesn't make them true,' he maintained decisively.

She could almost believe him, and yet ...

'You admitted it yourself when we were in Bundaberg,' she recalled, reluctantly. 'I said I knew what was going on with the pair of you, and you said in that case there wasn't any need for me to keep questioning you about it.'

A delightful smile etched its way across his well shaped mouth. I'm afraid I was being a trifle sarcastic,' he owned drily. 'Quite frankly, I'd become sick and tired of hearing what you kept insisting you *"knew"*. There wasn't—nor ever had been—anything between Melanie and myself, but you simply refused to believe me when I denied it.'

'Because you never did actually *deny* it,' she cried. 'You just kept telling me not to be ridiculous.'

'Well, what's that if it's not a denial?'

'It's a commonly used cover-up when someone's hit on an uncomfortable truth!'

Kirby stared at her incredulously. 'If you're about to tell me I went through four years of hell all because of an interpretative variation, I swear I'll wring your beautiful bloody neck, Alix!' he warned hoarsely.

'I was only eighteen, Kirby,' she offered nervously in excuse, shrinking a little away from him. He certainly looked angry enough to do as he threatend. 'And Melanie kept hinting how much you two meant to each other and how I'd only caught you on the rebound because you'd had an argument with her before you left for Canberra. I saw so little of you I was terrified you were going back to her. You always seemed to have time for her—all right, so it was only for business—but I couldn't be sure of that, especially when she kept saying otherwise. I was so frightened of losing you ...'

'You ran away instead!' He shook his head in disbelief and pulled her back to his side determinedly. Then, rolling on to his side and leaning over her, 'Okay, I freely admit I'm not blameless and I gave too little while expecting too much, and Melanie sure has a lot to answer for, *but* ...' An unavoidable hand tipped her face up to his. 'I'm telling you here and now, and even if I never do so again—unlikely though that is—I don't want you to ever forget, or to doubt, that I do not love Melanie, I have never loved Melanie, I have never even kissed Melanie, but I do happen to love every individual and collective inch of *you*, Alix Whitman—including that crazily confused head of yours—and I will continue to love you for the rest of my life! Now, do I need to interpret that in any other way, or is it fully understood as it is?'

The last remaining vestiges of Alix's doubts had all been swept away by the time he had finished and her aquamarine eyes glittered back at him enchantingly. 'I think a kiss might be just the thing to add a little extra conviction,' she dimpled.

No sonner suggested than carried out. Kirby's mouth covered hers with such sensuousness that her pulses were still hammering a hectic beat when he finally let her go some fevered minutes later.

'Convinced?' One dark eyebrow crooked with the provoking question.

'Almost,' she sighed and, laughing, ducked beneath a muscular arm when he made a feigned move towards her as if to continue his annihilation of her senses. From a safer, more calming distance, she quizzed softly, 'Why didn't you make any attempt to come after me when I left the first time, Kirby?'

'I was too damned proud,' he admitted heavily, regretfully, and slid on to his back to clasp his hands beneath his head. 'I'd managed to persuade myself into believing it was up to you to make the first move if we were to settle our differences. When you didn't, I self-righteously reasoned that proved how little our marriage meant to you and that I was better off without you.'

'Yet you unhesitatingly came to my aid when Mum contacted you.'

'My opportunity for revenge, to make you pay for the hell you'd put me through ... or so I thought,' he smiled wryly.

Alix nestled closer, relaxing contentedly when a strong arm secured her fast to his side. 'That's what I thought too. I was so upset at the idea of seeing you again they had to give me a sedative.'

'Mmm, I know,' he sighed contritely, but his ensuing grin wasn't penitent, it was lazily teasing. 'The doctor said it was the first time you'd shaken off your apathy for weeks.'

'Beast,' she charged lovingly, and pretended to sink her teeth into the firm flesh of his shoulder. 'Did you have to be quite so brutal in your approach to make me recover?'

'Nothing else appeared to work,' he laughed ruefully. 'I thought we may have been making progress the day we went to the mill, but as soon as we reached the beach afterwards you were so restless and edgy I didn't know what to make of it. Then, when I tried again at the Aylwards' party, you became so obstinately unco-operative I figured there was no hope of our ever getting together again.'

Alix glanced up a trifle shamefacedly from beneath long curling lashes. 'I thought you were only being nice to me because you wanted an easy divorce,' she pouted. 'And as for the beach ... well,' her shoulders rose lightly and she smiled with a provocative eloquence, 'I'd suddenly realised I wasn't as unaffected by my disturbing husband as I liked to believe and I was frightened to death of what might happen if you realised it too.'

Swiftly, Kirby's lithe body moved and she abruptly found herself imprisoned as he leant over her, gleaming eyes holding her slightly startled ones, a heart-stopping smile shaping the lips so close to her own.

'Shall I demonstrate what would have happened if I'd known, and nearly did happen anyway, but out of sheer frustration?' he drawled provokingly.

'No,' she protested, laughing, and halfheartedly seeking to evade his nearing mouth. 'You distract me so much I can't think properly and there are still things I want to talk about.'

'Okay, I'll wait,' he grinned, but not before he had claimed at least one hungry kiss from her responsive lips. 'Let's hear them.'

The sound of a heavy engine starting up in the street below momentarily diverted her. 'That must be my bus preparing to leave,' she mused, totally unconcerned. 'I'm glad I don't have the rest of the journey to do.'

'You shouldn't have needed to make any of it.'

'I know,' she agreed with a sigh, but as a chance thought came into her mind she looked at him faintly puzzled. 'You said you met Robert Miles in town this morning. I thought you were supposed to have left for that cattle sale on the tablelands.'

'And so I did,' he confirmed positively. 'But I was still trying to sort out your unexpected behaviour from last night. No matter what you'd said to the contrary, I was sure there'd been *something* different about you. It wasn't until we were almost there I happened to remember how unnerved you'd looked when I innocently asked if your plans were all set for today and I could start piecing everything together. I immediately turned back and found Clara in a frantic state after reading your note, but not until I reached town and bumped into Robert, of all people, could I fathom *why* you'd found it necessary to leave in such a hurry.'

A warm radiant light illuminated Alix's glowing features from within. 'So you *had* decided to come after me before you knew about the baby?'

'Of course!' It was a categorical statement which brooked no misunderstanding. 'I didn't intend to let my pride get in the way a second time. My main objective was to regain my wife ... the baby was a bonus.'

'Oh, Kirby, I love you!' she cried with delight, throwing her arms around his neck and pulling his head down to hers to kiss him ardently. 'I promise I'll never doubt you again.'

'You'd better not, my love ... or there'll be hell to pay, I can assure you!' he advised, not altogether mock-threateningly.

'And—and Melanie?' she had to probe. 'Did she really resign?'

'Oh, yes.' His eyes glittered disturbingly, his mouth a little grim. 'She'll certainly cause you no worries in the future.'

'What happened?'

'I took exception—extremely strong exception— to the remarks she had to make when I told her the reason we were turning back this morning,' he relayed harshly, and making Alix shiver unconsciously. Who knew better than she how demoralising her husband could be when he chose? 'There's no need for us to go into exactly what she said—suffice it to say she was apparently labouring under the misapprehension that I would be pleased to have you gone. When I made it plain that wasn't the case, she lost her temper and began accusing you of all manner of behaviour guaranteed to make any husband reach boiling point.'

'You didn't believe her, though?' Alix questioned anxiously.

Kirby shook his head reassuringly. 'I might have done if I hadn't known how much you disliked her. She can be very convincing at times,' he admitted wryly. 'But she slipped up badly when, in her desire to impress me with her truthfulness, she tried to make me believe you'd discussed some of these supposed happenings with her—in strict confidence, naturally —because I knew only too well you wouldn't have done anything of the kind.'

'Thank God for that,' she breathed gratefully. 'You do believe me now that she's always tried to cause trouble between us, don't you?'

'Uh-huh,' he assented regretfully, 'and I'm deeply sorry for doubting you too.' His head tipped to one side consideringly and he frowned. 'But what I really can't understand is why you kept accusing me of being interested in her without once telling me it was Melanie herself who was feeding you the idea.'

'In the beginning I was very confused, I—I'd known you for such a short time,' she began hesitantly. 'I think I was hoping for an outright denial from you ...'

'Which you didn't realise I'd already given.'

'Thereby making it unnecessary for me to show just what little faith I had in my ability to retain your interest. If I'd confronted you with Melanie's story, you might then have considered there was no need to pretend any longer and I would have lost you completely. I wanted to keep the little I believed I did have, rather than having nothing at all,' she confided wistfully.

'And instead I made it impossible for you to stay,' Kirby reproved with bitter self-censure.

'Oh, no, it wasn't all your fault,' Alix hastened to correct him. 'I could have made it easier on myself, and you for that matter, if I'd been willing to take an interest in something *other* than you,' she smiled impishly. 'I did make selfishly preposterous demands on your time which would have been ridiculous of you to have acceded to, and I didn't make any attempt to be a proper wife. Maybe if we could have had a baby then matters would have improved between us.'

'Perhaps ... but at least conception would have taken place in less callous circumstances.' His eyes closed and a muscle jerked violently against his taut jaw as he slumped on to his back. 'God! How does a man apologise for such insensitivity?' he groaned. 'I can mouth excuses like desire, need, jealousy, frustration, for ever and a day, but none of them come close to providing condonation, and I still despise myself for that night!'

Angling across his chest and feeling the heavy thud

of his heart against her own, Alix caught his face between her two hands and trailed her lips caressingly over his attractive mouth.

'Would it help if I said I'd already forgotten, and forgiven, the incident?' she asked.

'How could you forget?' His eyes flashed open to blaze vividly into hers. 'You've a pregnancy to keep reminding you.'

'Mmm,' she wrinkled her nose at him impudently. 'Isn't it wonderful?'

Kirby's arms crushed her to him tightly, his expression so adoring that it took her breath away. 'I don't deserve you,' he murmured huskily.

Alix couldn't agree, but she could—and did—lovingly proceed to demonstrate just how wrong she considered one male could be!

The Mills & Boon Rose is the Rose of Romance

Look for the Mills & Boon Rose next month

SUMMER OF THE WEEPING RAIN *by Yvonne Whittal*
Lisa had gone to the African veld for peace and quiet, but
that seemed impossible with the tough and ruthless Adam
Vandeleur around!

EDGE OF SPRING *by Helen Bianchin*
How could Karen convince Matt Lucas that she didn't want to
have anything to do with him, when he refused to take no for
an answer?

THE DEVIL DRIVES *by Jane Arbor*
Una was in despair when she learned that Zante Diomed had
married her for one reason: revenge. How could she prove to
him how wrong he was?

THE GIRL FROM THE SEA *by Anne Weale*
Armorel's trustee, the millionaire Sholto Ransome, was
hardly a knight on a white horse — in fact as time went on
she realised he was a cynical, cold-hearted rake . . .

SOMETHING LESS THAN LOVE *by Daphne Clair*
Vanessa's husband Thad had been badly injured in a car smash.
But he was recovering now, so why was he so bitter and cruel
in his attitude towards her?

THE DIVIDING LINE *by Kay Thorpe*
When the family business was left equally between Kerry and
her stepbrother Ross, the answer seemed to be for them to
marry — but how could they, when they didn't even like each
other?

AUTUMN SONG *by Margaret Pargeter*
To help her journalist brother, Tara had gone to a tiny Greek
island to get a story. But there she fell foul of the owner of
the island — the millionaire Damon Voulgaris . . .

SNOW BRIDE *by Margery Hilton*
It appeared that Jarret Earle had had reasons of his own for
wanting Lissa as his wife — but alas, love was the very least of
them . . .

SENSATION *by Charlotte Lamb*
Helen's husband Drew had kept studiously out of her way for
six years, but suddenly he was always there, disturbing, over-
bearing, and — what?

WEST OF THE WAMINDA *by Kerry Allyne*
Ashley Beaumont was resigned to selling the family sheep
station — but if only it hadn't had to be sold to that infuriating,
bullying Dane Carmichael!

Available February 1980

Doctor Nurse Romances

and January's
stories of romantic relationships behind the scenes
of modern medical life are:

TENDER LOVING CARE
by Kerry Mitchell

Stephanie loved nursing at the little Australian country
hospital, but why had Doctor Blair Tremayne suddenly
turned against her?

LAKELAND DOCTOR
by Jean Curtis

It was only when the beautiful Lena came to the
Lakeland village that Hilary understood why she had
stuck for so long to her job as Doctor Blake Kinross's
secretary!

Order your copies today from your local paperback retailer.

Mills & Boon Classics

The very best of Mills & Boon
romances, brought back for those of
you who missed reading them
when they were first published.

in
January
we bring back the following four
great romantic titles.

THE SPELL OF THE ENCHANTER
by Margery Hilton

Jo needed to enlist the help of Sir Sheridan Leroy, but
little did she expect that Sir Sheridan in his turn would
demand *her* help to further his own personal intrigue . . .

THE LITTLE NOBODY
by Violet Winspear

Ynis had lost her memory in an accident, so she had to
believe the dark and mysterious Gard St. Clair when he said
that she was going to marry him . . .

MAN OUT OF REACH
by Lilian Peake

When Rosalie asked the new deputy head, Dr. Adrian Crayford,
why he couldn't tolerate women, he replied that they were an
irritating distraction, and the more attractive they were, the
greater distraction they became. And Rosalie was attractive —
and attracted to him!

WHITE ROSE OF WINTER
by Anne Mather

It was six years since Julie had married Michael Pemberton
and left England — and Robert. Now Michael was dead, and
Julie and her small daughter were home again — only to
learn that Robert was now the child's guardian . . .